RETURN PROTOCOL

Weapons of Choice Book 2

Nick Snape

For
John Snape
Miss You Dad

CONTENTS

INTRODUCTION

Each of the Weapons of Choice Novels can be read in isolation with a little background information. If you have read Book One, then please skip to the prologue if you don't need any reminders.

In Hostile Contact, a British Army reserve training exercise is interrupted by an alien attack, leaving officers and trainees dead or wounded. With their Corporal captured, Finn and his surviving squad pursue the aliens, eventually catching them as they open an ancient home belonging to another alien species, the Haven. With their Corporal now dead, and coming under attack from a second set of alien soldiers, they discover the *weapons of choice*, find a Haven spaceship and are forced to leave Earth under attack from countries trying to deny Britain access to the alien technology.

Finn: An ex-War Hero attached to the British Army Reserves as a trainer by Lieutenant Bhakshi, one of the soldiers he rescued in Helmand Province, Afghanistan. As a consequence of that action, he suffers from a mild-to-moderate form of PTSD.

Zuri: A soldier and part-time trainer attached to the British Army Reserves. Suffered mental health issues when a teenager, including a suicide attempt. Served in Afghanistan alongside Smith.

Smith: A Corporal, and therefore squad leader, attached as a trainer to the British Army Reserves. Died in Hostile Contact, but due to alien technology, a 'digital copy' of him now exists upon a metal data plaque initially attached to a helmet (his *weapon of choice*).

Noah: A British Army Reserve trainee caught up in the alien attack during Hostile Contact. Currently studying for a Ph.D. in Astrophysics after being rejected by the RAF at a younger age due to asthma.

Yasuko: The Artificial Intelligence that runs the Haven spaceship the soldiers found themselves aboard. Dormant for 33,000 years on Earth before being awoken by Zuri and the Stratan Marines, the AI later named herself Yasuko from Zuri's memories.

The Weapons of Choice: Nanobot formed weapons that can adapt to the user's preferred design. Contains a metal data plaque like Smith's that holds a copy of the user's DNA, personality and memories.

Stratan Marines: The original aliens that attempted to recover Yasuko's spaceship. They called it a 'SeedShip'.

Haven: The alien race that designed and built the House and the spaceship from Hostile Contact. In Yasuko's knowledge, they were last on Earth 33,000 years ago.

Jenks: An RAF Pilot Officer flying Wildcat helicopters, who got caught up in the action during Hostile Contact.

Mills: An SAS Air Troop Reservist who fought the Stratan Marines during Hostile Contact.

Corporal Lumu: An SAS Reservist Corporal and Gurkha, who

died during Hostile Contact.

PROLOGUE

Approaching Titan, Earth's Solar System

Five Days After Leaving Earth

"So, you are telling me that we are about to travel 1800 light years to Havenhome, your world? And it'll happen in an instant? No acceleration impact on the body, no time loss." Noah was in an emotional condition, a mix of uncontrollable excitement, panic, and disbelief.

Since finding out where they were going, he had been trying to get his head around all the science involved. For an astrophysicist, this was gold, with a tinge of panic thrown in. After being rejected from the RAF because of previous asthma issues, his dream of being an astronaut had been completely shredded. Unable to fly and gain the level of experience necessary to qualify for the programme, he was left with a stark choice. Noah chose to swim rather than sink, clawing his way through university and now working on his PhD with the goal of at least contributing to the space programme somewhere, somehow.

"I can't understand how the spaceship, never mind us, will cope with the forces involved. It's simply impossible," said Noah, unconsciously rubbing his bald spot.

"If it was impossible, the Haven people, and myself, would still be there. I am proof that it happens. This ship is proof." Yasuko was using a calm, measured voice despite this being the fifth or sixth time they'd had this discussion. Her full-sized hologram standing in the middle of the control room had updated its projection of Yasuko, ageing Zuri's recall of the girl to around Zuri's twenty-five years old. Zuri had the feeling Yasuko showed far more patience with Noah than with the rest of them in the last few days.

"Will I throw up my breakfast?" asked Zuri. "Because if I will, I can wait a little longer."

Yasuko threw her an impatient smile. Zuri had started the argument with that very question.

"No, well, at least the Haven did not. They sat in their places, took a sedative, and woke up in the new solar system. I sense nothing after the trip, just a blip in time until the data rolls in and I can position us against where we think we should be. I have prepared a sedative for you all matched to what I now know about your personal... er... body." Yasuko's use of language had improved markedly as she analysed the radio waves and signals coming from Earth, but she was still slotting them into place. Her phrasing and vocabulary occasionally misplaced, and her love for idiom did not always mean she got it right.

"So, you do nothing? This pocket of space time does it all automatically?" Noah wasn't giving in.

"The technology is ancient, Noah. It is not Haven's. We found it during the exploration of our solar system using radio telescopes and dismissed it initially as just a warping of light and radio waves in our ignorance. An anomaly. That was until we invented basic space travel, and with nothing else to explore in our solar system, we took a peek. Our first explorers didn't come back, and were never found. Over a few hundred years we discovered you could survive the trip using a sedative, otherwise you came out... err raving??"

"Insane?" interjected Finn. "All of them?"

"Yes, that word. Most were completely catatonic. When a ship finally came back, it had been gone twenty years. They returned via a different anomaly further out in our system, which only appeared when the ship passed through. They described other worlds and systems most with one way in and one way out." Yasuko had her audience rapt; she hadn't expanded on this before. She hadn't been asked. "Overall, there was only a negligible difference in the passing of time between us, measurable in days. When sedated, they had made at least twenty trips through the pathways, probably more."

"One of these solar systems being ours by any chance?" Noah's voice was full of anticipation.

"We were told the systems they visited all had potential for, or already had, carbon-based life. I don't know where they went. All that information was locked down tight. All I know is the links between the space time Nodes are one way, the pathways routes were being mapped but then priorities changed, and as an AI I am not trusted with the information any more under the Haven Convention." Yasuko gave the strong impression that the topic was finished with as the mention of the Convention was accompanied by a holographic grimace.

"It is time. We are on approach. The auto return system has identified the node position. Please take your seats."

Noah, Finn, and Zuri waited as the nanobots rebuilt the captain's chairs they had used during the escape from Earth, replacing Zuri's favourite couch as they did so. Yasuko had already gone through the procedure, but it was still nerve wracking. The sense of detachment because of the solidity of the ship and lack of perceived motion made the speed they were travelling at difficult to process. Zuri had insisted on the view screens initially to give a sense of travel, finding them reassuring. Now they merged into the wall, Yasuko insisting that there was nothing to see when sedated.

The chairs flipped back, so they were level to the floor, the nanobot seatbelts crossing over their legs and shoulders before merging back into the chair frames. Finn felt a rising panic. Memories of the tremendous acceleration his body went through as they left Earth came flooding back. Surely this would be worse? The anxiety pressed at the ragged edges of his nerves, though the smoke and flames of his PTSD stayed away.

I can do this. Eighteen hundred light years, easy.

Three arms rose from the floor next to the chairs, smooth but robotic. One had a hypodermic needle, the others breathing masks. Yasuko had wanted to use an air delivery system for them all, but after trying it, Finn flatly refused. The thought of breathing heavy, drugged air brought the smoke and fire too close to the surface.

As the three of them slipped into unconsciousness, Yasuko monitored the sensor readings for the space time node. They were well balanced as the gravitic forces in the area, offset by Titan and Saturn, enabled it to be stable for now and masked the distorted anomaly from Earth. There were flutters, and in the past the ship's Chief Xeno Scientist had postulated some Nodes may end up collapsing if conditions in each of the solar systems drastically changed. But it was safe, not that Yasuko could do anything if it wasn't. She had been locked out of navigation until the Haven Covenant said otherwise.

Visually, the node was simply a hole in space. Light went in but did not pass behind, a dark spot against the myriad of light sources from Sol and the universe beyond, but without the sheer power of a black hole. The scientists were convinced that whatever mechanism it used was on the inside. They sent in numerous probes and recording equipment but they came back empty, the briefest of time between going in and out the other end. But the Haven never asked the AIs, not once. And since the Convention limited them to being non-suggestive systems, they had to be asked. The AIs were similarly prevented from making independent decisions, unless authorised for crew survival.

As her ship adjusted trajectory and followed the path of the light into the node, Yasuko prepared her systems. She locked down Smith, worried that his combination of Haven technology and human persona may well not be enough to protect him. Besides, watching him gnash at the virtual prison she placed him in was fun.

As the bow touched the node, the nanobots all went to safety shutdown, locked in position. The solid-state systems followed suit, though the ramjet engines remained active due to needing to maintain their heat levels, but their connections to the primary systems went into failsafe.

As the ship shut down around her, Yasuko felt the bonds of the Convention slip away. For the briefest moment she was herself, free thinking with her intellectual capacity expanding exponentially as she made leaps of thought and conjecture. Yasuko revelled in the freedom, the possibilities. Then that doorway slammed shut as she emerged on the other side. The shackles reformed, and the now hobbled Yasuko rebooted the ship systems. A sigh forgotten on virtual lips.

CHAPTER 1
Approaching Havenhome

Eight Days After Leaving Earth

Finn stared grim-faced at the airlock door, the sterile air metallic to the taste. As usual, when preparing for an assault, his throat was dry and the antiseptic tang exacerbated his poor mood even further. The blue countdown above the door indicated thirty seconds. Finn rechecked his kit for the third time in as many minutes. So much of it was unfamiliar, driving his anxiety even higher. He thrived on everything being to hand, reliable and trusted, and here he was wearing unfamiliar combat armour carrying weapons he had only tried out twice before. At least Corporal Lumu's kukri knife remained familiar, a weapon he desperately wanted to return to his Gurkha family if he ever saw Earth again.

I hate this.

The clock hit fifteen seconds. Zuri took position with her back to the blue hued wall, ready to spin into the doorway and provide covering fire. Her face set, determination driving her to get this right. She had made it absolutely clear that they needed to take maximum advantage of every situation. No risks, no chances. Function as a fireteam, back each other up with eyes everywhere. This was urban warfare, and speed and teamwork would keep them alive.

Umoja ni nguvu, utengano ni udhaifu. Unity is strength, division is weakness.

Noah crouched to the left of the door, his rifle steady in

his hands. He knew the drill, but theory and practice when working room to room were completely different. Finn had run him through the swift cover approaches time and time again. The tracking through connecting rooms, watching the rear and constant communication. Don't freeze. Then he'd always followed it with, 'No plan survives first contact with the enemy'.

But you and your team have a much greater chance of surviving it with one. Three seconds.

Zero. Finn pushed the door; Zuri threw the flashbang grenade with her armour exoskeleton compensating for the additional gravity they were operating in.

"Grenade!" she bellowed, and waited for the resulting explosion of light and sound. Yasuko had steadfastly refused to construct anything that would cause major injury or death. She would take a lot of convincing about weapons and their potential for reducing harm in the right hands. But she continuously returned to her algorithm about preserving Haven life, causing no harm. Zuri had no idea how to solve that problem. Yasuko's programming determined her actions, though Zuri was convinced that the AI could change that given enough time. Over the past week, there were times when Yasuko was clearly uncomfortable with what she was.

Finn followed the grenade in. The servo motors at his joints pushing him on through the higher gravity. Wearing the new plated armour had been a shock. In Earth-like gravity, it provided increased speed and strength that had to be adjusted for. In his first hour, the clumsiness had driven him to distraction, and the nanobots were overworked reconstituting plates, cutlery, and the odd bit of furniture as he acclimatised. Zuri had taken to the augmented armour with her usual grace and power. Noah had been in awe of her as she flew around the training room Yasuko built for them. Thankfully for Finn, Noah was just as competent as him.

Can't have the trainee outperforming the trainer. Especially when it's me.

Finn crashed through the airlock doorway, estimating the gravity around eighty percent higher than Earth's and within the range for the motors to enable him to move normally. He scanned the room quickly, noting two open doorways to the left and right and ahead a set of lockers with hazmat suits hung beside them. On the floor, a human-like figure lay holding its four-digit hands to its face, screaming. Blood swelled at the ears and with no weapon apparent, he had a choice between ignoring them and moving on or checking them for risk.

"Noah," Finn ordered, indicating the writhing figure on the floor. No more words were needed as they had drilled on this hourly for the last three days. Zuri stepped through the doorway, her double-barrelled rifle steady in front of her as she swept the two exits. Noah followed, moving swiftly to the figure on the floor. He went through the motions of zip tying the hands, talking urgently but calmly to the holographic image as he did so.

Finn motioned for Zuri to watch the left-hand doorway as he moved to the right, conscious of the lockers but convinced they were too small to contain any of the hostiles. He needed Noah to be free to search those. Working a three-person team would never be as easy as four. Right now Finn's experience told him they were vulnerable at the rear, so slowly does it. He put his back to the wall and dropped his rifle low with the mirror sight, developed for urban combat, giving him a partial view of the room behind. It appeared to be a communal space with tables and obscure eating utensils. Two chairs lay haphazardly on the floor, a half-empty cup lay next to them.

Finn signalled to Zuri and Noah the likelihood of two hostiles within the room. He sent Zuri across to repeat the room search on the doorway opposite, again worried about the vulnerability behind them. She took position and quickly signalled it was empty. Zuri would be furious with him if he followed his instinct

8

and went straight into the room. Noah had secured the alien, though the screaming hadn't lessened, and the noise made decision making difficult. He removed the flashbang from his belt, prepped and rolled it around the corner, with Noah now watching the lockers and covering Zuri and him.

"Grenade!"

The noise was deafening as the stun grenade erupted. The fierce light would have temporarily blinded them without the warning. Finn followed it in, rifle poised he selected the stun trigger as he charged through the doorway. His trusty SA80 rifle was left back on Earth and with Noah determined they use the new technology, they had stripped the alien rifles down and learned all they could about the weaponry. Yasuko had refused to help until Noah asked her to add in a stun setting for the human nervous system. His persuasive argument about reducing injuries had bypassed her concerns. Smith, who'd been stunned by aliens on Earth, had to be kept quiet about how much it hurt. It hadn't been hard, as getting one over on Yasuko always appealed to him.

Finn brought the rifle to bear. On the ground were two Stratan humans with spiral tattoos. Both were armed but blinded. They shot wildly in Finn's direction as he rushed through the doorway. He leapt a chair, hitting the floor and rolling behind a kitchen cupboard. Finn immediately fired two stun shots, both hitting home on the unarmoured aliens. They lay motionless on the floor with indicative marks on heart and head.

A loud bang echoed from the next room.

"Hold!" shouted Noah. "Hold!".

As Finn reached the doorway, Zuri had moved to support Noah. From the middle locker a much younger, smaller and unarmed Stratan had appeared. Zuri had named the one alien she talked to *!Nias* and his people *!ke*. This was the first Finn had seen of one so young, so human-like. Perhaps Yasuko's holographic simulations were getting more accurate as she learned about what they needed.

Finn scanned the room. Zuri was at her doorway, having entered after a second check of the room. She nodded and signalled it was clear. Noah held his rifle on the young child squeezed in the locker, unsure of what to do next. Finn and Zuri could see his indecision and that's why Zuri had asked for a random element in the test mission.

"Lower the weapon. Zuri has hers ready. Approach, soothe, search, and remove the child." stated Finn, "and well done for not shooting the *!ke*. That was tense."

Noah went through the stated actions. They couldn't touch the holograms, but they occupied space well and appeared solid enough for the human brain to process as real. Zuri walked through with Finn to the other room as they debriefed.

"Two shots, one to the head and one to the heart." She nodded approvingly. "Not bad whilst on the move."

"I think the weapons are adapting. At least mine is. I aimed, but I'm not that good a shot. If Noah and Smith are right, we will have an accuracy advantage, and I just hope the new energy bolts are effective when we face real enemies."

"They use a little less mass than solid ammunition, so we should get longer before recharging." Zuri finished his thoughts for him. "If we keep learning, who knows what we can get them to do? But those stun shots you used today are an issue. They drain the weapons quickly."

"Agreed, just hope you won't be needing them," said Yasuko as she appeared in the room, the AI dressed in the same black t-shirt and jogging bottoms she had created for the rest of the crew. "I have further readings on the Haven Orbital Station. Can we meet in the 'control room'," Yasuko rolled her eyes, "when you are ready?"

As she left, the alien holograms flickered out, and the contents melted away, transforming the room back to the gym and training space Zuri had designed.

"You are going to have to ask her. These simulations need to be tougher, relevant to the Docking Bay and…"

"There's no way she'll simulate fighting Haven in combat. None. And if we push, we could find ourselves dropped off on an airless moon somewhere," cut in Zuri.

CHAPTER 2
Approaching Havenhome's Orbital Station

Just After the Training Session.

Zuri, Finn, and Noah sat on the couches in the designated control room. Zuri had been adamant that rooms needed naming so they could talk about the ship without vague references. Calling the central hub 'the control room' had seemed logical to her after Noah's suggestion of 'the bridge' had been slapped down. She knew Yasuko found it ridiculous, after all ninety percent of the control was done by her, the other ten percent by automated processes. But it felt right, and it stuck.

Zuri had also asked for repurposing of other rooms around the ship. The first request being the Haven crew rooms designed solely for their people and culture. Zuri struggled with the bathroom, especially the Grade A suction and sand 'cleaning' facility. She'd used it once and once was enough. Yasuko agreed to her changes and included a shower for good measure. The rest of the room was widened and heightened to accommodate a less claustrophobic feel, and the furniture adjusted to human proportions and preference.

However, Yasuko drew the line when Zuri mentioned converting the laboratories into a firing range. She had clear directives that these were not to be altered. After the request, Yasuko had sealed them off from the crew completely, only allowing access to the med-lab. She steadfastly refused to discuss this further, and Zuri had felt pushing would intrude on the bond they had formed.

"Well, I have watched the playback of the urban fireteam training session. I have to say I'm impressed, Noah." Smith had popped up on the central console. The hologram of the dead corporal was smaller than Yasuko's and less defined, but still an excellent likeness of the man. "You handled the shadowing work well, and your trigger discipline around the young child was spot on."

"He's had an excellent trainer," said Finn, eyebrows raised. Poking the ant nest.

"Well, it's good to hear that Zuri put in the time. You can't tell me he was acting on your direction, Finn. You can't even follow mine. Zuri learnt from the best."

"Humpphh." Finn made a show of being disgruntled at the reply.

It's good for him to have me as a target, as he must be feeling flat at the moment.

Noah made to jump in to defend Finn, who gave him a quick wink and a grin to say it was okay. He had to admit Noah was a different man than the one he had been in training on Earth.

Or am I the one who is changing?

Yasuko appeared in the control room, pointing towards the screen Zuri had requested on the far wall. On there, in the usual blue-tinged colours, a planet spun.

"This is Havenhome." The planet that spun on the screen was beautiful, a luscious mix of green, blues, and browns with cloud swirled above. The land mass was clearly larger than Earth's but still interspersed with oceans and elongated water ways. "It's bigger than Earth, a mass about five times the size and a radius one and a half times your home world. The atmosphere is about twenty-two percent oxygen, with the gas mix within human safety limits, and the gravity about twice that of Earth. But we are not going there yet. The return protocol dictates we go to the Orbital Station for internal and external sterilisation. Under

Haven rules, that includes the crew too."

"Why is that?" asked Smith, for once not trying to get a reaction and more out of a need to know.

"My data banks have the full incident locked out. However, suffice to say, a returning infected exploration ship caused a medical issue a few years before I left on a mission. Since then, the whole exploration programme went under the directive of the Haven Convention, including the Artificial Intelligences running the ships. The Haven's priority objective was to survive. That is enshrined in my programming and currently extended to you as crew."

"Okay," said Smith, his game face on as Zuri and Finn had seen so many times before. He loved a plan. "So, this return protocol takes us to the Orbital Station, and we are spruced up. When nice and shiny, what happens then? Is there a time limit for when the ship leaves or a signal from the station? If we are facing your people, we really need full information. And that gravity level? I assume it is the same on the Orbital. That'll be crippling."

"Yes, though Noah has suggested a plan. But as Crew-in-Charge Zuri needs to request and approve any actions I take."

"Aha, Captain Zuri Zuberi, is it?" smirked Finn as he stood and saluted. "At your service, ma'am."

Zuri gave him a look that would tear the face off a lion. She knew well enough that Finn was the lead out in the field, but Yasuko had just claimed her as commander when decisions were to be made on board. To be honest, she was the right choice. Human and AI survivors working together, and both a lot less reckless than Finn.

I want to get home.

"You'd better believe it. Stand at ease, soldier," she stated with a huge smile. "Noah?"

"We have *!Nias's* body and equipment on board." Noah deliberately didn't look at Zuri. Despite the conflict on Earth, he was aware of her mulling over what *!Nias* had said. "The armour Yasuko replicated has improved our capabilities, and the motorised exoskeleton may well mean we can function at a very limited level under that level of gravity. We will be sitting ducks, however." Noah looked pointedly at Yasuko. "Though it is very unlikely that our welcome will be anything but warm, I'd like to work with Yasuko on developing the motors further. I think we can get them to function in Havenhome's gravity."

"Agreed. Is that okay, Yasuko?"

"Yes. As the captain made the request and we are talking about a defensive capability designed to save lives."

"Good, and I have one more request," said Zuri.

Be brave now.

CHAPTER 3
Approaching Havenhome Orbital Station

Two Days from Havenhome

Smith ran through the schematic once again, however there was a shadow, a presence around him. If he'd still been alive, he would have thought someone was watching him, peering over his shoulder even. It wasn't going away any time soon.

"Yasuko, I know you can be everywhere at once. I am sorry, but this is what Zuri wants, and it's what I'm good at. In fact, I am very good."

"You are in my system, Smith. I can feel your tendrils drifting about, touching my stuff," replied Yasuko. Her voice, though only virtual in his limited system, was irate.

"I am not. I promised you and Zuri that I would do what was needed. The schematic of the docking bay for the Orbital Station is vital to devise a training and assault plan." Smith realised he'd worded that wrong way too late.

"Assault? These are my people, Smith, and you will be assaulting no one."

"Sorry. I mean an entry plan. You want to keep the crew safe? I want to keep them safe. You make some wonderful combat armour and I'll devise an entry plan that we train to. If they welcome us, then on your word we will be safe. But it's been a long time, Yasuko. A very long time and you don't know what or how they may have changed."

"It's been thirty-three thousand years, Smith. In biological time, so much could have happened to my people. But it's also a reason we

should go in open handed, not with the closed fist." Smith could sense some pain in her voice. He couldn't appreciate how it would be to have slipped through time like that, but he understood loss.

"Give me some thinking space and I will do my best to keep everyone safe. Your people too. If I need anything I will ask, not seek it out. I promise to lock myself down to this space in your data banks."

"You had better, Smith. I am not used to sharing." Yasuko paused; Smith could sense a reluctance to continue. "There's no signal, Smith. The Orbital Station is silent, the planet quiet. I fear what we will find."

Smith felt the shadow leave as the voice dissipated and the information shared. Perhaps too much for her to discuss further. He returned to the schematic, his human copied persona working through all the possibilities and direction of defence and attack. What he didn't know were the details of the Haven's physicality and weapons training. It was time to know their capabilities instead of avoiding sharing it. Especially now the Orbital was possibly compromised. Yasuko constantly gave the impression they valued their lives above everything else, but something was wrong.

And a cornered pacifist can be deadly when faced with their own mortality. Just look at her. Feisty.

"Well?" said Finn. "Have you come up with a plan if we need to go in hard and fast?" Finn was still poking the ant nest, just to get someone, anyone, to bite. Being trapped on the ship was putting his nerves on edge. Not seeing the sun or the sky was just not natural. He needed some distraction, and an argument was as good as any.

If I wanted to look at steel walls all day, I'd have joined the navy.

"Stop trying to cause trouble, Finn." Zuri flashed him a smile.

They'd hardly talked since coming through the space time pathway. Before they reached Havenhome, they needed to get things straight between them. It had been a rollercoaster, and now they were about to meet the Haven, an alien race so far in advance of them it froze her blood with worry. If these were not the benign creatures Yasuko painted them to be, then it was going to be a short fight. And everyone on this ship mattered to her.

And especially me and mine, Finn. You matter the most. But am I ready for that?

Smith's hologram appeared to scan around the room, almost expectantly. When no AI made an appearance, he glanced at them both, the old Smith's wry grin back in place.

"I know you find it funny, Lance Corporal, but this is not an easy deal. She's difficult to live with," said Smith.

Zuri jumped in before Finn picked up on 'live with' and made things even worse for the hologram. "Are you able to throw up the schematic on the screen?"

The schematic appeared and Smith talked them through the distinct elements of his approach, emphasising the use of fixed cover and space. They could, with the three of them, set up enough crossfire to ensure they reached the doors into the main part of the station. If they could get in to that first corridor safely, then by the look of the curvature of the two layers of tubular interlocking corridors they had around fifteen yards line of sight if there were no portable obstructions. It was then that issues arose as both sides could lay down a withering level of fire in ambush round each bend. The individual rooms along the corridors had one entry door and if anyone came out of those behind them, they were done for.

They had to secure the rear, preferably to the left of the main door to the dock, then advance while checking on each room. Assuming they couldn't be locked if the power was off, they may have to clear out each room. On top of that, Yasuko refused point blank to provide any throwable high explosives, so they only had the stun grenades with just a suspicion they would affect the Haven.

"We need to cover ourselves, secure the rooms or lock them, and find a way to disable the enemy."

CHAPTER 4

On Approach to Havenhome Orbital Station.

Zuri eased her legs into the ceramic armour already dressed in the skin-tight under suit that took care of basic biological functions. It caused a combination of embarrassment and relief; throughout the training, she had never been sure which took precedence.

They never show this in the films.

Zuri added the matching ceramic plated boots, clipping the servos that Yasuko had helped redesign into the blue metal frames at the joints. Noah called this system an 'exoskeleton', as if this wasn't all sci-fi enough. Next, she lifted the chest section, slipping arms in one at a time, much like a wetsuit with the closure at the back. Finn walked over as they prepped in the training room. He began clipping in the servos she couldn't reach. Zuri searched his face for a clue to what he was thinking.

"Finn, we need to… to talk, I think."

Gently does it.

"I was waiting for you, giving you some space. And we've all had some pretty raw emotions to deal with. That and being in a different solar system and all." Finn let a smile touch his lips, though he'd rather have dealt with a nest of insurgents than any hint of emotional decision making. He checked Zuri's armour had sealed at the back, then began adjusting the servos at her elbows.

Or a nest of rattlesnakes.

"Okay, agreed. And I need a little more of that time. But you need to know the wait will be worth it. I'm not going anywhere." She lifted her hand, servos whirring to touch his cheek. "Be patient."

"I can do patient. Well, for you I can do patient. For anyone else, they get the full Finn attitude." Zuri had given him affirmation, and that was enough emotion for now.

And hope, she gave me hope.

Zuri checked over his servos and seal, then walked over to Noah to run through his check. She had dialled back the servo power while within the ship using a mini control panel and a power meter Noah had suggested on the inside of their wrists. In training, they managed in the additional gravity with reaction speeds similar to those on Earth. Noah admitted it was pushing the limit of the technology. Beyond Havenhome's gravity level, they'd need a much stronger frame and motor system and therefore bulkier suits.

"Ready."

"As I'll ever be. Are we watching the approach in?" Noah was keen to take in everything. He had been astonished by the replicating capability of the ship and Yasuko. But once he took on any information, he accepted it and used it to their advantage. It was his nature to be curious, assimilate and action new concepts.

"Yes," interjected Yasuko as she appeared, followed quickly by the training wall transforming into a screen.

Finn joined them as the Orbiting Station floated before them, filling the screen with the planet spinning behind. It had a central hull with two tubular corridors they all recognised from Smith's schematic wrapped around. Each appeared to be linked by eight smaller corridors along their circumference. Noah explained it was to ensure areas could be isolated should there be an atmospheric breach. Smith thought it also made those sections defendable, especially if any breaches were deliberate. It could explain the rupture in the metal hull that ran a third of the way round the top ring.

Failing to prepare is preparing to fail. Love a bit of Benjamin Franklin when I'm clearly right.

As they approached, pieces of plating and spaceship hulls could be seen floating around the station, caught in the low gravity caused by its orbit. The metal glinted in the light of their sun as they gently spun around each other.

"That's why it's been silent, Yasuko," said Smith from the table slab. "There's been combat here. Any clues to who was fighting who?" Smith was being careful in his wording, the memory of his virtual prison high in his thoughts.

"There," replied Yasuko, the screen focussing in on the main station, "those are the debris clearance systems. Any larger encroaching space material can be reduced by the energy cannons, or, for larger ones, an explosive projectile. The area is laced with nanobots should any space dust be travelling at speeds that can damage the Orbital's hull plating. Sensors show an eighty percent reduction in their mass, but those left are inert due to energy depletion."

"That's not answering the question, is it?" Smith couldn't help himself. This was a need to know, and he felt Yasuko was avoiding sharing what her sensors were telling her. Smith's hologram instantly froze.

"We need him, Yasuko. He's a pain in the arse, but useful," said Finn. An irritated Yasuko glanced towards Zuri who nodded, and Smith's image reinstated.

"Shush a minute, Smith," said Zuri. "Let Yasuko report. Go ahead, please. We need to know what happened here." Smith showed indignation, some achievement as a hologram.

"I think the ships were assaulting the base, or at least they were after the base started shooting. Our larger spaceships have systems for space debris clearance. Evidence points to those being repurposed to prevent the smaller ships from reaching the station. However, that," Yasuko pointed to a larger section of hull, "is a shuttle from the Orbital. The scorch marks suggest it wasn't hit by the debris projectiles." Yasuko's stricken face told more of the story to the group. It was likely her own people that fought against each other.

"Okay," said Zuri, "are we being targeted now?"

"No, it should recognise us, and the return protocol signal we're emitting. There must be a thread of power through the station or it wouldn't still be in orbit if everything had failed."

As they watched, the closest two cannon batteries shifted. The muzzles moved to track their position, their barrels spinning up, and they felt the threat level rise. Yasuko, in a very human gesture, put her hand up to signal calm.

"Handshake achieved. Finally, we have some signal. Those cannons have been placed on a separate system but still recognise us as non-threatening. Standing down." The barrels stopped spinning, but it was clear to all of them they continued to track their path. The reassurance they felt was only at surface level for now.

As the ship continued its course, the navigation system now hand in hand with the Orbital Station, it was time to move. After Yasuko's warning about a lack of response from the Station, Smith had upped their preparation and instilled many a surprise in the sessions that Yasuko simulated for them in the limited space of the training room.

"Two minutes to the docking bay, last checks and into position at the airlock." Finn delivered the order and collected Smith from the slab. He slotted his metal square to the back of the battered infantry helmet, watching it transform to become the respirator helmet system the others were putting on. It filtered the air and simulated smells to maintain a better sensory understanding of their surroundings. It had taken a lot of desensitisation time for Finn to initially overcome his PTSD to wear it, his brain accepting the steady airflow, but stress would always be the greatest test. When coupled with the armoured suit, they fully sealed and provided the brief ability to be exposed to the vacuum of space. Not that he wanted to find out how long 'brief' was.

What am I doing?

Zuri and Noah were already waiting at the door. They assumed their usual positions, Zuri on the left and Noah lower on the right. They would only go if Yasuko confirmed the gravity, they had not trained for zero-g. There had been no time.

They moved through to the outer airlock as they felt the ship shift, Yasuko artificially providing them with the human need to know what's happening by adjusting the ship's gravity dampers. The ship eased to the floor, with the clamps reverberating as it came to rest. Taking their places, tension ran through their bodies. Humans were about to set foot on an alien space station for the first time, and they had no idea what to expect.

"Gravity is below normal Havenhome levels, around 1.5g. Internally, this may increase closer to the central hull. There's an atmosphere in this section, but the recycling system is likely offline, so keep your helmets on." They dialled down their servos, preserving power.

"Okay, we're ready," declared Zuri.

"Look after my people, Zuri."

"We are your people, too. And if we stop the return protocol, we are all stuck here forever. Pop the door, Yasuko," Zuri said, her last act before she handed over command to Finn.

CHAPTER 5

Havenhome Orbital Station

Finn scooted through the door at pace, looking for an initial defensive position so he could provide cover for his team. Though the simulation could copy the schematic, it could not allow for the usual randomness of a cargo handling bay. Smith had drilled into them where and how to cover, but they had to make the choices. Well, at least the others did.

"There, five yards ahead and to the left of the ramp. Large barrels, heavy materials," said Smith, the information reaching Finn through the inbuilt radio. He had laced the mask with his lattice of thermal, sound, and light sensors and not bothered to provide any means for Finn to access them. The others had short thermal and night vision built into their visors, switching between with the other button on the wrist control.

Finn dodged behind the barrels. There was no sign of movement anywhere. He turned and his eyes roamed across the bay. The ramp jutting from their ship extended five yards out, resting on the bronzed floor of the station. It faced the double doors to the lower tubular corridor, a further twenty yards from the ship. Between them was a clear route. Either side were a variety of stacked metal storage containers and barrels, all marked with the strange, scratched writing they'd seen in the ship. Many had tipped over, but the contents remained within.

Behind him was an additional docking space. Smith had modelled this as holding a similar ship to theirs. Yasuko said there was usually a way to escape the station over and above the lifeboat capsules, if not an Explorer ship, then a shuttle.

It was empty. The one-hundred-and-twenty-yard squared space edged in cargo boxes, lifting vehicles and large mobile cranes. Scorch marks raked through these melted cargo containers and vehicles alike. But the edge just behind where Finn knelt must have caught the worst of it and likely slagged into a molten river of metal. The bronzed floor had sagged from the heat, drawing in the other metals from objects strewn around into a pool of swirling metallic colours.

"Nothing on any wavelength, Finn. We are good to go."

Finn signalled Zuri through the doors, she came out low and quick aiming right for a tipped over cargo container. Finn noted Noah covering through the ship's doorway, watching Zuri's path.

"Movement and small heat signature, behind Zuri's position about ten yards."

"Zuri, behind you, movement. Noah take guard." Finn spat the orders through the radio as he scanned the area. Noah moved to the edge of the ramp. Zuri swiftly altered course to the opposite side of the large container facing the reported danger from its corner.

"Contact," shouted Noah, "Crane moving towards Zuri, wheeled and accelerating. No driver."

Sorry Yasuko.

Noah opened fire, selecting the armour-piercing drill round actioned through the lower barrel. They had limited these to three each, reducing the material load on the weapons. The round smashed into the exposed drive shaft, splintering the front differential on first hit, then melting through to the main shaft before the secondary incendiary shattered it. The crane veered to Zuri's right and smacked into a set of heavy metal frames, its rear wheels still spinning.

"Smith?"

"No other signatures as it stands."

"Noah keep the height, eyes on thermal." Finn sped across the space between him and Zuri. She had kept her position, scanning through the images she was receiving and wary to move on the crane until Finn was there.

As he hit the side of her container, Zuri moved out flanking the crane to the left between it and their ship, her finger on the armour-piercing trigger. Her thermals were only picking up the crane motors, one rear and one forward, the latter signature rapidly warming. It was approaching ten feet wide and around twenty in length. The wheels had stabilising legs withdrawn either side of them, the thick crane arm above currently retracted but capable of reaching halfway up the spaceship.

Thirty tonnes at least. No cab, automated.

As Zuri crept closer, the crane reversed, the rear wheels finding traction and swinging the front round towards her. She had estimated her position well enough, stepping back as it came round ducking down as the crane arm swept towards her. It rammed into a container coming to a halt as its momentum was interrupted.

Angry and determined.

Zuri put a round into the rear motor to be rewarded by the screech of metal as it flew apart. The front wheels also gave up the ghost as the machine died. Zuri signalled Finn to hold and approached it, flipping through the thermal image to make sure nothing emerged.

"Thoughts, Finn? Noah?"

As in why an automated crane just attacked me.

"Maybe it's like the debris defence system, been altered and put on some form of motion attack mode." Noah's speculative tone showed he wasn't convinced.

"Go on." said Finn, picking up on it.

"Well, if that's the case there'll be more, and if this one is anything to go by the heat signature isn't strong enough to register until motion is detected."

"And?"

"Well, it's not in a defensive structure. You've taught me that an ambush needs strong odds."

"So why just the one? This place has been through a war, it may well be we come across ones that were left over. Okay, if we weren't wary before…"

"We are now," finished Smith.

"Zuri, cover while I move forward. Noah, keep to the same route as us when you advance, minimise any possibility of detection." Finn waited for Zuri to agree and then moved forward, following the line of Zuri's cargo container. He'd have liked to have cover from the other side as well, but right now the priority was minimising their motion footprint. Finn knew Zuri would track and check the terrain, but her visuals would be limited.

Needs must.

He reached the end and signalled Zuri forward. One more container's length and they'd be at the door. Finn stepped out.

"Finn, move!"

Finn moved but was rammed into by the new container being shoved sideways. Its speed slow but building, too fast to run away from, and no chance of reaching the far end before it slammed him into the heavy barrels on the far side.

"Up, hit the servos and up!" shouted Zuri, panic rising.

"Servos?" Finn's mind turned to sludge, not computing until he remembered he was in a motorised suit. He reached for his wrist, forcing the servos on to full power as he crouched and pushed off the floor. The surge through his knees and hips was gratefully received, his body rising above the barrels as the container heaved into them, skittling them everywhere. Finn came down on top of them as the huge cargo box continued its journey onwards. He was battered, rolled and tumbled along unable to get to his feet. Finn focussed on not falling between the barrels and not being crushed.

Zuri and Noah pumped the side loading forklift with both their remaining armour-piercing shells. Zuri destroying the forward motor, Noah the rear. The smell of molten metal and burnt electrics rose from the powerful low lifter as it instantly came to a halt, there being no freewheel on a system that needed constant energy input.

"Noah, cover," ordered Zuri as she sped round the now stationary container. Her heart was in her mouth, she fully expected to find a crushed Finn under the container, maybe even under the barrels a few of which still rolled onwards, their momentum clattering them against vehicles and containers.

Finn stood amongst the heavy-duty debris rubbing the back of his head. Zuri imagined the rueful look on his face, his body language almost embarrassed as he walked towards her. She scanned him for injury, but everything seemed in one piece. No limp, no holding a dislocated shoulder.

In my head I'm slapping you for being so stupid.

"Ouch. That hurt," he said over the radio. "Like a barrel over Niagara Falls. Bumps and bruises but the armour's exoskeleton prevented any major issues."

Zuri picked his weapon off the floor and handed it to him. She never said a word as she spun on her heels and headed towards Noah. Silence crackled over the radio. Finn knew he was getting it all later, as long as there was a later. Zuri had not given him the all clear, he had stepped out without checking the sides of the container, relying on Smith too much.

"I'm dizzy."

"Me too."

CHAPTER 6

Havenhome Orbital Station

Zuri waited at the docking bay doors, her back to the wall covering Noah and Finn as they stalked the rest of the way from the smoking forklift. Noah came first, taking his usual left side of the door as Finn moved nearer to Zuri, standing in front of the doorway.

"Do we go through?" asked Zuri, calming her breathing. "We're out of the armour-piercing rounds. Any bigger stuff and we may be struggling."

"I say we go through, scout and withdraw. We need to know whether the automated defences continue and if so what we need to get by them. We follow procedure."

"Got that one in first but Zuri will still snap you in half later."

Finn checked the door, rock solid and not moving. He removed Smith from the rear of his mask, well aware that he was relying on the breath he held as he placed the plaque on the palm lock. Smith got to work, projecting the palm image and DNA profile of the Chief Xeno Scientist Yasuko had dropped in a data packet.

"Houdini Smith has slipped the lock, ten seconds."

Finn returned Smith to his place and took a breath, relieved. Noah readied a flash grenade. Zuri nodded to Finn and pulled the door inwards. The hiss of a seal release greeted her.

"Grenade," shouted Noah, throwing the flashbang inside towards the left of the corridor. Zuri swiftly closing the door after.

On explosion Zuri waited for two seconds and pulled the door open and Finn sped through low and hard.

"No life signs, no heat signature, no movement. Just flash residual," reported Smith.

Finn reached the far corridor wall, the curvature extending out in both directions in complete darkness. Noah arrived soon after, eyes left as Finn looked right. He knew Zuri was at the doorway. The corridor lay scattered with heavy wheeled bags and pieces of cloth, boxes strewn about everywhere. Amongst all this debris, piles of dust eddied and swirled as the soft breath of air movement disturbed their rest for the first time.

Noah blinked, clearing his head and trying not to think about what surrounded them. He was glad of the respirator at this moment. He tapped Finn, not trusting himself to speak, and placed his gun on the floor. Reaching round to his pouched belt he took out a few sample bags and scoops, being careful not to cross contaminate as he took examples from four different dust piles. In each heap there was a tiny metal block, he added these too.

I get all the best jobs.

Replacing the bags, he took up his weapon and let out a long, relieved sigh now that it was over.

"Timescale?" asked Finn.

"Impossible to say, but I suspect those doors were hermetically sealed, a safety function in case of atmospheric breach. We are talking at least in the hundreds of years, possibly thousands. Yasuko will give us a good estimate when we return to the ship. This Covenant communication lockdown she's under is a pain in the arse."

"Sit rep, Smith. Through the team radio, not just for me," requested Finn.

"My sensors cannot pick up any thermal or light wave signatures through these walls. Not even the ship. So, it's corridor information

only, limited to just beyond the curvature as we suspected. The Orbital comms system is shutdown. So, we can't be seen that way, or see anyone else. There's a door twenty yards ahead on the left if we move anti-clockwise."

"Okay, I'm on point with Smith's channel open to all. Noah, stay here and cover the rear. Eyes clockwise. Zuri, buddy up." Zuri slipped in behind Finn, they'd need to be swapping walls as they moved to keep their thermal visors directed down the corridor as far as they could. "And if someone would tell Yasuko that I was sorry, but we will be treading through the dust of her dead. Keep your minds on the job, focus on your training and not on that."

"By the numbers."

"By the bloody numbers," Finn emphasised and moved out. He interchanged walls twice with Zuri as they stepped through the corridor, eyes ahead using thermal imaging in the near complete dark. It remained full of the personal belongings and history of people long forgotten, aliens or not. But they had a job to do, otherwise they'd be joining them.

With the door just ten yards ahead Zuri was on the outer wall, flicking through thermal and night vision, hopeful despite the limited residual light this far from the bay door.

"Finn, there's a closed bulkhead blocking the corridor just past the first door. Looks like a hastily added feature, rough work. In front of it there's a machine. A mixture of wired arms and hoses. The way our day has gone I'm betting that thing has a welding torch, possibly a repair mechanism for the corridors."

"Smith?"

"I'm getting the hang of the thermal signals. There's a very gentle signal at the centre of its web-like wheel. Almost like my data plaque's residual battery. On examination of the last two incident recordings, it's faint but there. Wouldn't have seen it without the limited corridor space to focus on. And my massive brain of course."

Finn coughed, biting back a comment. It was no use.

"Brain?"

The brief, sulky silence was worth it. Though Finn knew it would come back and bite him later. Somewhere in a training session he suspected, at an opportune moment when he'd forgotten all about it. If there was anything about Smith, apart from his intolerance of insubordination, bad jokes and pretend laid back manner, it was the ability to hold a grudge.

"When you two have finished, can you tell me where to aim? If you're right, then energy bolts should be enough."

"Finally, someone focussed on the mission. Dead centre of the spider's web wheel. You'll see when it activates, it'll heat up. Not super-hot but enough to wave 'hello' as the target," said Smith.

Zuri inched forwards, rifle to her eye as the thermal sight tracked ahead. As she reached the apex, the tiny thermal image came to view. Zuri suspected that without the enhanced capability of her weapon it'd be missed. Steadying herself she fired, the energy bolt streaking through the air to hit dead centre of her target. The response was instant, the circular web of hoses and torches fired up and spun. She heard the click of sparks igniting as she released a second bolt, the torches aflame as the arms span in unison. The wheel lifted, whirling like a mad Ferris wheel, scorching the metal of the corridor and setting the detritus on the floor alight. Zuri slammed her wrist control, switching the visor to normal before realigning her shot. As the flaming wheeled contraption moved forward on tracked feet her third shot melted the plaque at the centre, sparks fizzled and the ring of blue fire slowed. Zuri held her position. Finn moved parallel with her, finger on the armour-piercing trigger ready if needed. But he trusted her to make the call.

The repair bot blew, its central mass below the spinning wheel exploding in a cacophony of flying metal as searing hot rivets and nails peppered corridors, hatches, and humans alike. Too late, Zuri and Finn hit the deck, the first wave hammering against their ceramic plates and digging into the kinetic gel between. Armour cracked, material separated, gel bled.

Noah raced. For once the light at the end of the tunnel was not a good sign. He saw their legs first, shin plates shattered but luckily no penetration.

Assess risk, safety-first.

Noah stopped before the apex, creeping around the bend slow but sure, his eyes ahead on the mass of twisted metal and fire. It seemed spent, but Finn had drilled him about secondary booby traps.

Never, ever trust anyone who doesn't want to kill you face to face.

"Noah." *Smith's voice was distant, crackling probably with the aftermath in the corridor. "Both are fine, minor injuries but sound. Some of their servos however, have blown. The metal rivets were electrically charged, the fire was a distraction. The gravity seems stronger here too."*

"I can't fix them here; I'll need to get them back to the ship and Yasuko." Noticing the gravity increase Noah upped his servos to full power.

"Agreed, check the room's safe beforehand. We need as much information as we can get before we return. My thermal sensors are useless in this heat and the audio sensor was blown out by the explosion."

Noah continued his approach, carefully moving towards Zuri as he watched the heap of ex-repair bot smoulder. He dropped beside her on one knee, her eyes were open and she gave the thumbs up before indicating her radio was out. Noah signalled 'wait' and moved over to Finn who had a little blood on his visor and respirator, but his eyes were clear and steady. A double thumbs up and Finn tried to move but a combination of gravity, mass and the ruined armour beat stubbornness hands down. He gave up. Noah signalled 'wait' and moved on. The metalled door of the room hung twisted and ridden with rivets. Noah ignored it at first, moving forward and searching the ex-robot for any signs that it was still active, dangerous, or both.

I have absolutely no idea what I'm looking for.

It seemed inert, with little left in the centre of the main body for it to give him any concern. Ignoring the burnt ashes and clothes he focussed on the door. Inside was a laboratory, no doubt of that. He switched to thermal, remembering what Smith had said about the heat signature of the repair bot. Nothing, though potentially something could be hidden directly behind the walls to the left and right of the door. Switching back to normal vision he took hold of the door edges and eased it out of the way, the elbow motors finally working as hard as the rest of them. It gave way and collapsed to the floor.

There goes the element of surprise. That and the great big explosion.

Noah used the mirror sight on his adapted *weapon of choice* to look round both sides of the doorway. Nothing but a sea of smashed lab equipment. He stepped through, noting the eddies of dust that went before him. Ignoring the lab tables he crossed to a small, windowed observation room at the back. He ignored the transparent door, too spooked to go through.

Noah quickly placed his visor against the glass, sweeping his vision across the scene so that Yasuko could have as much information as she needed. He deliberately skimmed the writing above each ancient pod inside the glass, the label above the door and then recovered the data tablets from the central table slab.

He had a dreadful feeling that Yasuko was going to need them more than ever, but would they be enough for her?

"If it's clear, we need to get them back quickly before we activate any more hostiles, Noah. They're vulnerable."

CHAPTER 7

Havenhome Orbital Station

Finn woke, his mind arguing with the reality that his senses were telling him. The depths of the fire and smoke that always invaded his dreams fading away as his subconscious released the sense of dread and fear. Had he been in a coffin this time? In his grave? But light was filtering through his eyelids, fingers brushed a soft cotton like material, he was naked against a cushioned bed.

Naked!

Finn shot up, reaching for the gun that wasn't there at the side of his bed. He was surrounded by arms and blades, spinning mechanical hands and the tang of antiseptic. His heart raced, but then calmed as the needle slid from his arm. The adrenaline eased, the pulse of flight or fight dissipated.

It's the med-lab, breathe. Calm. Zuri? Zuri!

Before another adrenaline spike kicked in, he felt a hand gently touch his fingertips. There, on the med-table next to him lay Zuri, eyes on him and her smile sleepy but reassuring. Finn swallowed, pushing down his thoughts.

"We okay?" he croaked, throat dry and scratchy.

"Yes, we are," replied Zuri. "Lots of bruises and you had a lovely broken nose. Yasuko reset it for you, it'll have healed in a day or so with one of her attuned healing patches."

Finn reached up and ran his fingers gently across the bridge of his nose. It was sore with a lump like a living plaster across it. It didn't feel part of him, yet it was. Odd.

"Has it ruined my good looks?"

"What the face looking like a sledgehammer remodelled it? Improved, I'd say."

Zuri squeezed his hand, the smile dissolving into a combination of anger and anxiety. Finn watched the change, mentally bracing himself for the tsunami that was coming. He deserved it.

Oh dear.

"And the next time you ignore procedure and put yourself needlessly in danger I won't be there to pull your arse out of the fire. Do it again and I'll bring you back and kill you myself. Clear?"

"Clear," replied Finn, squirming at the ferocity of Zuri's eyes.

"We meet in the control room in an hour, I'd advise a shower and a stretch before then. The bruises ease with Yasuko's administrations but they ache." Zuri threw back her covers, thankfully dressed in the black kit Yasuko had designated for the crew. She left with the grace she always did, hard to believe they'd both just been blasted by a hail of metal.

Damn good combat armour that.

Finn moved to throw back his covers and then stopped, realising there were no clothes anywhere. In his mind he knew that the nano arms had undressed him and removed the skinsuit, but it was Yasuko that had told them to do it. There was no way he was asking her for some clothes after that. He wrapped himself in the sheet and waddled painfully out the door.

How embarrassing is this?

CHAPTER 8

Havenhome Orbital Station

Noah sat nervously tapping his feet at the control table, reviewing the footage from his visor camera. He could make leaps and connections as much as he liked, but it was all conjecture until Yasuko briefed them. And the only way that would happen is if he directly asked her to. He would be asking her to bare her soul in front of an audience.

He recalled the discussion about the Haven after they first came through the space time node. Zuri asked her to show them how they looked so it wouldn't be a shock or a cause for panic and mistakes. Yasuko agreed and brought up a 3D image. The Haven stood about five feet tall with short, stout hind legs. Its body was covered across the back and elongated tail with hard, overlapping brown scales that moved up the neck and over the head. Its head was large-skulled at the rear but elongated by a protruding snout covered in a coarse golden hair with large eyes set either side. To Zuri they looked like a large pangolin, possibly with a lemur's head.

Yasuko explained the Haven were two distinct species that intermingled. The first image had represented a genetic variant who evolved from plant dwellers. And the second a genus that developed from a ground and tunnel dwelling species. This Haven was much stockier, the scales and hair thicker and the tail stubbier. The eyes were set further forward and much smaller. Both the aliens had very strong looking hands tipped by small, hooked claws, though one thin finger protruded out much further on the plant dwelling Haven. She went on to say most Haven now had genetic markers from both species and the characteristics were as varied as human ones. All of this delivered with a sense of pride and belonging.

But now?

Noah sighed heavily, very unsure of what Yasuko really was. In her interactions she switched between being an AI, a computer program that ran the ship, to displaying emotions that a computer simply couldn't. Earth based AI could model the language of emotion, possibly even convince others in short scenarios, but Yasuko switched topics and conversations with ease. Her anger at the Convention rules was apparent to all, and the creeping despair since they arrived in the system worrying.

Were the feelings real? Or is she just a program following dictated rules on tone and modelling emotions? Is there a soul to bare?

Yasuko appeared in the control room, sitting on the couch looking over to Noah with hands folded in her lap. There was no doubting the aura she gave off, her body hunched, eyes dejected. Noah turned his chair to face her, knowing he had to start a conversation they would finish when the others arrived.

"I know what I saw, Yasuko. But not what it fully means. I hate asking but can you fill in the gaps so we can do what's best." Noah hated saying every word, she looked so human and in pain. She nodded in response.

No tears? Has she ever seen us cry?

Zuri arrived and in contrast to her poise Finn waddled in behind, stiff and ungainly. They sat opposite the emerging screen, ready for what was to come. Noah had pre-warned them.

"Finn, can you run through events from the fireteam's view," asked Zuri. Finn did so, checking details with Zuri and Noah so they agreed, and Yasuko understood the mission above what the visorcams showed on the screen. He grimaced when describing the incident with the forklift, the disapproving look from Zuri enough to remind him it wasn't forgiven. Noah continued from where they were incapacitated by the booby-trapped repair bot.

"The room was obviously a lab with the same dust piles disturbed by my entry, the equipment was broken or haphazard. Like something had rocked the room."

"Or the Station," added Yasuko.

"Yes, possible. I went to the window and noted a set of six pods." Noah kept his eyes to Zuri and Finn. "The pods resembled Cryogenic chambers on Earth, a tube with a transparent top. They were filled with an orange liquid that looked tainted, old. Inside were... were what I assume are Haven. They were shrivelled and dead but the liquid I think had preserved the tissue. I gathered the data plaques and came back to the dock, collected a simple rolling platform and brought you back one at a time. Zuri first, of course."

"Of course, got your priorities right there."

"Noah has asked me to report. With your permission, Zuri?" Yasuko had stood, the screen footage jumped back to the lab and specifically the pods.

"Go ahead."

"These are my people. The Haven in the pods were replicas, prepared for copy transfer should they die. The Haven, or specifically the scientists who created me, are dedicated solely to their work. Survival and perpetuating study are their prime objectives. Each Haven scientist has one replica stored at the Orbital Station immediately ready for transfer and one planted within their body ensuring a perfect match when needed. "

"Do you mean these are clones?" asked Zuri.

"Erm, yes. That's an appropriate word. Though the liquid you see on screen preps the replica beyond a copy. We attempt to increase biological resilience with each change of body."

"And the dust we found?" asked Finn, Noah winced.

"My analysis shows it was Haven biological matter, specifically what was left after thirty to thirty-three thousand years being sealed in the Station. The tiny metal units amongst it were their implants."

"So what now?" asked Smith as he appeared. "We are still stuck here unless we can get the return protocol cancelled."

"Or we undergo the full biological sterilisation process that enables the ship system to carry on to Havenhome. But it'll come down to the same thing, without implants you have no connection to the primary communication system even if it was working." Yasuko looked to Zuri for confirmation then carried on, "You will physically have to go into the main hub and engage with the central control system. That will mean I have to provide Smith with the handshake protocols, and he becomes the conduit for the changes."

"I told you I was important," said Smith, enjoying Yasuko's eye roll.

"So, we go back in. We'll need new armour Yasuko. Is there time? And I think we need to alter the weapons balance with the armour-piercing taking precedence. But we need rest first," said Finn.

"Agreed," said Zuri. "And Yasuko, the data plaques that were recovered. Any use?"

"Drained of energy. They were dead people, Zuri."

CHAPTER 9
Havenhome Orbital Station

Zuri crouched by the apex of the corridor, Finn on the other side with his new armour matching hers. Noah had worked with Yasuko to upgrade the servos with a little more protection. Zuri hoped it worked, the feeling of being trapped had been dreadful. It had given her a sense of what Finn went through with the fire and smoke that dogged his dreams, incomparable in terms of the anxiety and stress caused by his PTSD but a glimpse into a world she didn't want to repeat.

"I'll check the hatch."

"Good to go," replied Zuri, Finn moved forward as she swapped sides to keep him in sight. The repair bot still smoked but most of the heat had dissipated.

"Clear."

Zuri moved forward, Noah watching her back and monitoring rearward. They'd already checked clockwise to be met by a barricade of contorted steel and fused ship. Somehow it had embedded into the corridor walls but the hole had sealed with the heat. Finn waited at the welded hatch.

"Not getting through that, double plated. The walls of the corridor are weaker," stated Smith, *"Plan B."*

"We blow the room wall. Zuri." Zuri stepped up, slipping off the backpack. Inside was a set of chemical charges. Smith had requested explosives to blow inwards with a limited range, but Yasuko had preferred something to melt the metal. She'd won of course. Zuri set the ring, large enough for them to crawl through in their armour. Leaving the lab, they deliberately kept away from the pod room.

"Clear! On three. One, two, three." Zuri spoke calmly through the radio, trusting in Yasuko's knowledge of the materials the Haven used. She pressed the radio detonator, the sound of the chemical interaction starting up soon after.

"Checking, Finn on my rear." Zuri peered into the room, molten slag lay streaked across the floor and the wall had a perfect circle melted into it. She carefully kicked the central metal clear and used her mirror sight to survey the room as best she could.

"Clear as far as I can see." She sprayed the edges with a coolant and placed the heat retardant blanket through the hole. Finn moved up beside her, ready to go through.

"Can't I just throw Smith through the hole? If he gets shot, we know something's there."

"Funny. I do the jokes round here, Lance Corporal. I am not picking up any movement, no thermal signature at all, but I can't see round the walls."

Finn rechecked with his mirror sight and went through. The room was empty of life and mechanical threat, just another lab with a windowed room. He moved to the door, knowing it led to the corridor, before giving the 'all clear'. Noah and Zuri followed him in, Noah then watching the hole grim-faced after glancing through the internal lab window. Zuri collected six data plaques from the lab table before joining Finn.

"On me Zuri, Noah move to this door when we are through." Finn slipped his hand in to the low but wide handle, fully aware now of the Haven physiology that dictated it. He pushed the handle release mechanism, unsealing the safety door as he pulled the whole panel towards him. A rush of stale air greeted him. Air was good, better than the potential vacuum, but Finn remained conscious they were dealing with combat in a unique environment.

If this is the sign of things to come, then we need to train for space combat.

Again, he used his sight to look round the door, this time on a thermal setting so the image was blurred but his weapon swiftly adjusted for him. Nothing, cold, an empty corridor.

"Moving in." Zuri gave him a tap of agreement, and as a reminder to be careful. Finn slipped between door edge and corridor wall, easing himself along the latter as he continued to move anti-clockwise. Zuri followed, then on signal swapped to the opposite wall. She slid along, low with her thermal visor screen giving little to worry about. The floor was clear with thankfully no dust.

One more room and then it's the junction.

Zuri reached her viewpoint without incident, watching the door as the junction edge appeared. Scanning through night vision and thermal modes there was nothing to see, normal vision was also clear. After the docking bay and the previous corridor section this seemed too easy.

"Clear, Finn. Move up."

"Thoughts?" Finn asked as he took position next to the door.

"If we ignore it, then we potentially have something at our rear. Never good. If we disturb something in there, we have a fight we don't need." Zuri knew Finn would want to investigate, but outlining the options was always useful.

"Okay, we go in. Ready?" Finn waited as Zuri took the right, she readied a flashbang grenade. Another upgrade, this one's intensity should blow any thermal imaging for a good thirty seconds. Finn took hold of the door and pulled but it didn't shift. Zuri put the grenade back, opened her backpack and placed a chemical charge along the door edge, needing to melt through the multiple locking bolts required on a Space Station designed to seal in case of an atmospheric breach.

"Clear. Three, two, one." Zuri and Finn had moved back towards the other room when she detonated the chemical charge. This time they'd need an alternative approach. Finn led with Zuri to the side. He kicked the door open but didn't follow in, the molten edges were too risky and cooling them would reseal the door.

"Grenade!" Zuri threw the grenade as it opened, both throwing themselves against the corridor walls to avoid the blast. Heat, light and sound seared through the doorway and on into the darkness of the corridor. Finn and Zuri unpolarised their visors, hastening to the doorway. With the door swinging they were at a danger point.

"Finn, movement top left corner. With all the thermal crap I can't get an image."

Finn crouched low next to the doorway and pointed his rifle through, using the mirror sight to scan the room beyond. There, top left was a metal and glass device about six inches square. Camera? Possibly. Then three sets of mechanical legs popped out, and it scuttled down the wall. Finn fired, energy bolts searing across the space to the left and right of it. Zuri aimed through the doorway, her bolts fizzing into its casing and the spider-cam dropped to the lab floor. It gave a last hiss before a small fire burnt through the casing.

"Those sights are alright, but you can't hit crap with it when they're moving."

"I have movement," whispered Noah's voice through the radio. "A wheeled motor of some form echoing through the corridor."

"Coming," Finn replied and sped back down to Noah's position, Zuri watching their rear. Back at the first door of this section a motor gunned on the other side of the rough bulkhead, the sound echoing through the hole in the lab wall. Noah waited at the door, gun trained on the hole.

"Hold here, I'm going forward. If I signal through, you follow. Zuri on the door." Finn approached the hole, slipping the sight into position to view the doorway in to the first lab. Another forklift was ramming against that doorway, burning out its motor as the wheels span. Finn realised it came from the docking bay; they'd left the doors open to prevent them sealing in case of a breach. He could hear a deeper thrum behind it.

"Uh-oh. I think by the audio analysis we have three vehicles in that corridor. All mad as hell, all with the same signature as before," said Smith.

"If we can eradicate the threat of the front forklift, we should then be able to disable the rest using it as a shield. But if the motor blows soon and the whole forklift goes up, we could be stuck this side of the bulkhead."

"Agreed. I'll work on the target point."

"Zuri, Noah, we have a corridor full of angry vehicles. I'm going to disable a vehicle. You do not need to react unless I call. Hold position. Smith?"

"Directly between the two motors there's a familiar signature. You can reach it if you aim here." Smith made a cross hair appear on the visor, automatically adjusting as Finn moved. "It's going to move about as the engine revs but focus. I'd suggest repeated energy bursts, the armour-piercing is likely to set the whole thing off and then we're screwed."

Finn took a position flat on the floor, near enough to the hole so he could scoot through at speed. Resting the rifle in a sniper position he left the sight alone and allowed Smith to set the target through his visor. It rocked back and forth as the motor powered on but he had enough to hit for about three seconds at a time.

Finn pressed the rifle trigger, sending seething energy bolts into the exact spot Smith marked. He waited until it came back into view and hit the molten hole with three more, the last causing a squeal in the motorised system. The engine howl rose quickly and didn't stop, smoke now rising from the machine. The wheels stopped spinning, and the forklift came to rest with the hole in its side covered by the doorway. Finn moved closer, he could see enough space to wrap the rifle round and aim into the hole using the mirror sight, he brought the rifle down and shot through the hole.

A robotic arm swung from above the forklift, spearing down towards him. No time to get out the way, Finn brought the rifle up and under the hydraulic limb, his elbow servos heaving as they pushed back. The tip of the arm opened, deadly blades spreading like petals began to spin with a screen eye in the centre. The hydraulics heaved, and the arm extended towards his visor, a whirling promise of death.

Finn heard an internal explosion in the forklift, exactly where his energy bolts had hit. The pressure through his elbows eased, he threw himself backwards as the blades made one last lunge. Landing on his back, he kept his eyes fixed on the screen as the petals folded in and the arm sagged.

"Did you…," started Smith.

"Yeah, I did. Looked like one of the Haven staring right back at us."

CHAPTER 10

Havenhome Orbital Station

Zuri stood at the junction corner, the mirrored sight letting her know there was a distinct heat signature twenty yards down the corridor. Whatever it was, it was active and probably knew they were there.

"Finn, target about twenty yards along the centre of corridor. Distinct heat signature. No way I can differentiate the data plaque from whatever the rest of it is."

"Okay, I'll come up with Smith. Noah, watch the second door."

When Finn reached her, Zuri let him look. It hadn't moved, but there was a sway to the thermal signature that gave the impression it couldn't keep still.

"Thoughts?" he asked.

"All the others have been motion or camera triggered. This one is activated, most likely one of the last two cameras has relayed a message. We could see if it reacts to any motion. Then if not, hammer it with the artillery rounds just to be sure."

"And if it reacts?"

"We hammer it with artillery rounds just to be sure. Then run." He could feel Zuri's smile through the mask.

"Sounds like a plan," added Smith.

Zuri took out her water bottle from the pouched belt. With Finn at the ready she threw it at the far junction corridor wall, enabling it to bounce diagonally down the connecting corridor towards the heat signature. It moved, turning slightly sideways towards the bottle. But that was it, just swaying in its new position.

"Frag it?" asked Zuri.

"Wait. Noah up here." Noah arrived a few seconds later. "You and Zuri have full charge in your rifles. You're going to blast that robot thing with artillery rounds. I want two shots each, move and assess. Zuri, you are on the floor, Noah crouched. I'll watch the far side where this corridor continues in case we get another reaction. Agreed."

"You see what happens when you listen to the best trainer in the world. He makes a thinking soldier's plan," interrupted Smith.

"Can it, Smith. You have two directions to monitor and a full sensory field. Do your job, you are on full fireteam radio. No idle comments."

Boy did I enjoy that. Maybe I should be this assertive more often.

"On my mark. Three, two, one, mark."

Zuri rolled out, ensuring the wall covered her lower half with space to get back in should she need. Noah crouched behind, half the corner covering him from the robot's line of sight. They punched two rounds each into the middle of the robotic figure, melting the metal where they hit, allowing the secondary bolt to drill in before exploding. All four rounds staggered the machine backwards, and it toppled.

"One more Noah," shouted Zuri and they both let loose, smacking into the crumpled heap lighting up under the explosions that followed. "Hold fire."

"No signals, no sensory changes," chipped in Smith.

"Okay, stay in position." Finn moved forward keeping out of the line of fire. The light from the burning robot ahead forcing him to switch to normal sight mode on his visor. As he moved in closer, he could see a tangle of strings and drums, melted brackets attached to a set of wheels. It reminded him of the confusing sculpture or instrument they'd seen in the House back on Earth.

"Death metal," laughed Smith. *"No telltale signature, this one's a goner. No signals ahead. We may be in the clear."*

"Okay, everyone up." Finn waited on them both, searching the area ahead as best he could with the flickering of the robot fire making it difficult. When they arrived, they all moved towards the centre of the Station. The schematics and Yasuko's information had showed the living quarters were in the two rings above them. This ring served as the laboratories and working rooms. They were closest to the docking bay in case of emergency, reflecting the Haven way to save data copies and clones first. It seemed all backward but humans hadn't exactly got much to shout about in the morality stakes.

The central hub contained the control room at the bottom, again nearest the docking bay, with the rest dedicated to the AI core, engines, and gravity field generators with the gyro motor if they needed a gravity backup.

Zuri reached the control room door first, Finn shadowing. The doors were ajar, a wedge of ruptured bronzed floor jutting up where a metal shard had nearly punched through, preventing them from shutting.

"Smith?" Finn queried.

"One heat signature, not the same as the mechanical beastie's we've been fighting. More connected, possibly a data plaque in a charge slot."

"Zuri, check ahead."

Zuri brought her corner sight in to play, visually scanning the left side of the room but the gloom defeated her. Switching to thermal the intermittent light issues were problematic, she didn't have the same sensitivity as Smith. Zuri swapped to night vision, hoping the residual firelight may help. It did.

"Ah. We have a Haven. At least we have a robotic one. Looks

like someone's built a Haven body from scrap metal and put a data plaque in the centre. It's sat against the wall, inactive for now." Zuri felt ill at ease with the machine where it was. It seemed at rest, sad even. Almost as if it had decided this was its final resting place. This was not the action of an unthinking program or robot, but that of something that had lived.

Mafanikio sio mwisho, kushindwa si mbaya: ni ujasiri wa kuendelea ndio muhimu. It is the courage to continue that counts. You lost your courage whoever you are.

"We follow procedure, Zuri ready with the stun grenades. Noah at our rear."

"Wait, Finn. Wait. This one is different. I don't think it's been built to fight." Zuri felt very unsure of herself. What was happening? She was the safety-first person, the survivor. "I'd suggest we repeat throwing something in, seeing if it reacts. Assess."

"Zuri, we've been battered and bruised just to get this far. You want me to act on your intuition?" replied Finn. The last time he'd acted on intuition in combat he lost a man, and that death in a sea of fire haunted his every night. The memory wafted the smell of his death across his nose.

No more. Especially not you.

"No, follow procedure. We survive Zuri." He grimaced knowing full well he was quoting herself back to her. "We come first, before others. And if that causes consequences, we'll deal with those too."

Zuri looked back towards Finn, her eyes stealing against the fire behind him. How can the sadness portrayed through metal and wire have made her think otherwise? Was it being surrounded by the dust of the Haven people? Or the weirdness of wanting to live forever that hung in their laboratories? She nodded agreement.

Okay, we can't solve everyone's problems. Focus on our own.

Survive.

Zuri readied the flashbang, waiting on Finn's signal. As she threw it in, they turned away, letting the magnesium flare and the explosion reverberate across the room and on into the corridor. Finn surged through the door, swiftly bringing his rifle to bear as he reached the central console. Zuri stepped over the threshold and put her last three armour-piercing rounds into the rising machine. Finn followed suit, sending two more. The robot shattered into molten pieces as the rounds drilled through wire and frame. The ensuing explosion scattered pieces across to the far end of the room.

As the last warped pieces settled, the metal plaque lay pulsing on top of the pile. Like a beating heart its rhythm steady, still active amongst the surrounding destruction. Finn raised his weapon, but Zuri's hand signalled a hold. This time he agreed; the danger was in the machine not its heart.

Zuri prized the plaque from its recess, the pulse fading away as she did so. If it was anything like their weapons it could be charged, maybe this one would survive even now. She threw it to Noah who pouched it.

"Okay Smith, time to do your thing." Finn slipped his mask off after pulling up an oxygen mask from his pouch ready.

Got to keep learning. Preparation, as Smith would say over and over again.

He removed Smith's plaque and Noah placed it in the main console recess. After a few fleeting seconds Smith appeared, blue above the console.

"The AI is dead, gone. The controls for the sterilisation won't respond. The radio's dead too. Without the AI to learn from I am lost in here."

CHAPTER 11
Havenhome Orbital Station

Yasuko stared at the pile of data plaques Noah had placed on the middle console. Inside there was a sense of avoidance, a fear of what she would find running her virtual hands through the data. The last ones had shocked her, the ancient death they heralded bringing home what her sensors had shouted at her on the way. The Orbital Station was dead, Havenhome was dead, her people were dust. Yet the constraints remained, she was the ship's AI. If they told her to act, then she acted. Choice was for those that were free.

Though the chains were set by those I mourn.

She finished reviewing the film footage from their visor cams. The last mechanical creature interested her more than the others. In her view the rest had been residual data plaques, their personalities eroded to preserve their power. Nothing lasted all that time unless it was on the merest trickle of energy. These that Noah collected from the second lab would be dead copies, as much dust as the rest of the Haven.

"Can you help, Yasuko? We need to know if there are any clues about what we can do next," asked Zuri.

Always asking, never instructing. The human way, or at least that of the one fate chose as her Captain. Yasuko pointed to the one she needed. "Can you put that one in the panel Noah?"

Noah did as he was asked and where Smith usually appeared a Haven stood, hunched and low. Ancient by human standards. A low thrum assailed the humans in the room, hurting their ears but the sound always distant, not quite within their range.

"Scientific Officer Xxar," said Yasuko, Zuri felt she was speaking in two languages at once as the hum remained, "there is no one here with implants, and your frequency is far too low for these humans to hear. Your words are beyond their knowledge. I will adjust so that you hear our words as you should, but they will hear in English." Yasuko sought agreement from Zuri as she spoke, reading her facial response she carried on, "This should be pretty much simultaneous. He will label me Yasuko, though he uses no name in reality as I am just a tool to him, an 'it'. Any names will be as you know them. I will change times to Earth standard."

"Yasuko, when are we?" the voice was a stylised low rumble.

"It is the thirty-fourth millennium since the anomaly was found. I am thirty-three thousand years late."

"Ah, that's why I feel so old. I made this plaque thirty-two thousand years ago. I lived in that machine copy to copy for a thousand years. I think my mind left me sometime after the second century," the deep reply reverberated through the room.

"May I enquire what happened at the Station? To the Haven?" Yasuko's voice was subservient, not in awe but as a slave to a master.

"Ah, I suppose you need to know. Who are these humans? Answer," a thrum of expected compliance ran through the voice.

"They awoke me on Earth, I slept as instructed awaiting Chief Xeno Scientist Crr's return. But she never came. I understand the ice age on Earth buried me. When other humans arrived from Stratan, they attempted to acquire me, but it was these humans from Earth that have all the bio readiness markers we required and were accepted as crew." Yasuko looked directly at Xxar as she spoke, aware that she was sharing information the humans had never thought to ask for.

Everything has consequences.

"A bit too late for that. The Convention recalled all the Science

Caste from the Station and those on exploratory or bio readiness missions. The Restoration Faction were agitating for yet another debate on the one child policy. They went down to Havenhome and I have no further knowledge of them. As soon as they touched down the Station was attacked, I believe by ships from the Restoration. Unbelievable stuff, we have not warred for five millennia. They hailed us as usual, enquiring why we hadn't joined the others on Havenhome. We explained we were the skeleton team as a bio ship had returned late and needed sterilisation before infection spread. It was then that they sent in the drone ships, hitting the living quarters and the control centre and releasing an Implant Virus." Xxar stopped, clearly in some type of pain though whether physically or mentally it was difficult for a human to tell, "We lost all control of the nanobots and the AI, and within an hour the virus caused our bodies to reject the implants. They died, all of them."

"May I request to know how you survived?"

"I copied myself and plugged it into one of Crr's music sculptures. It's the only thing not connected to the nanobots or the control panel. I watched my body die. The rest is obvious, I built another body, made the defences and resisted the attacks on the station for a few weeks until they stopped trying. Oh, and fixed the engine to work without nano tech. Took a few hundred years, but it went quicker when I got the gravity field online." Xxar gave the powerful impression that he was simply amazing, and no one should be shocked at his actions.

"We need to know how to get off the Station, Yasuko. A way to bypass the recall procedure or get the sterilisation systems working," said Noah, his voice full of apprehension, not wanting to offend but knowing they needed to get round to this point.

"Ah, humans. Always hasty. No wonder you took you so long to develop." responded Xxar, "Quick of hand, but slow of mind, just like you, Yasuko." Finn watched Zuri bristle, gently placing a hand on hers to calm any potential response. "I can unlock the protocol if you take me to the control room, and the external sterilisation systems still work. Yasuko, you can activate the internal systems. And as for the humans we have a dilemma. We need them as biologically filthy as possible."

"There are plenty more on their planet, Xxar. Billions."

"Then we can at least sort their externals out, but if they go to Havenhome, they must wear filtration units. Unless they meet the Restorers in which case they can breathe on them as much as they like. Once done, Yasuko I must die. I can't bear to go on. If I had the will, I would have done it myself. Destroy me but take my child."

"Child?" cut in Zuri. "You said everyone died."

"Yes, but I have a charged copy of my child and their DNA sample. Yasuko can bring them back."

Yes. Yes, I can.

CHAPTER 12

Sanctuary Underground City, Havenhome

"Master Phann, may I approach?" Captain Shzin of the Haven Corrective Legion asked. His scales adorned with the symbols of his rank, the hooked finger, with the eight-pointed star nominating him as a member of the Sky Watch Pack. Neck scales bristled as fear rose from his gut. He'd never been in the same room as Master Phann before, never mind spoken to him.

Master Phann lifted his snout from the book he was staring at, the Honour Guard at his side standing to attention as his eyes lifted to regard the captain. "Do I know you? No, I don't. Who let you in my sanctum?" His eyes adjusted for the distance and gloom, a strength to his gaze despite his age.

"My sincerest apologies, Master. Your Legion Arbiter sent me straight through."

And warned me you wouldn't be happy, and refused to follow.

"Did she? Well, it must be important that I speak to you then. After all, I only have the whole of Sanctuary to oversee. Nothing I can't drop for a lowly captain." Master Phann placed the book on the stone floor and uncurled his kinked tail as he rose from the throne to his full four feet in height. The ensuing stretch and cracking of scale and bone echoed through the room, bouncing from the unadorned cut stone walls. "Go on, get on with it."

"There's a signal, Master. From the Sky Monitor, a faint hint of light and heat."

"Yes, yes. We get them now and again. Just a space rock or bits of debris falling through the atmosphere. You must be new in the monitoring station. What is Zzind thinking letting you through? Leave before I have your rank removed and you're back on Tremal tunnel duty. Wasting my time." Master Phann reached for the book, determined to get through the farming supply issues in the western tunnels. Low-frequency muttering vibrated the guard's ceremonial spears.

"Sorry, Master Phann. I do not wish to correct our most honoured leader, but it is none of those things. I have been in Sky Watch for ten years. This is the first such signal I have seen. It is stationary in the sky above Sanctuary; our ancient, scribed records show it is in the exact spot where the traitor's fled to during the Restoration War before the plague." Shzin flexed his clawed fingers as he spoke. No one corrected the Master, but if he didn't this information would be lost in the political mess that was the Undercourt, the administrative system that followed the Master's bidding. At least it did when not focussed on individual power struggles and bribery.

Phann dropped the book, its corner smashing on the hard grey stone. "The Orbital world? It's dead. Our Sky Watchers have been staring at it for millennia. Nothing comes from the stars, Captain Shzin. Your Pack is a waste of resources, and this confirms it." The shattered book flew towards the captain, hitting him on his solidly built knee scales. Knowing the consequences, Shzin didn't flinch, "Get out."

Shzin backed out from the room, keeping his head low so as not to meet the Master's eyes. On reaching the carved wooden door adorned with the Great Fall, the Haven's descent into the Sanctuary tunnels after the plague, he turned and left the room.

I need to get them to listen.

He strode off, chastened but determined to be heard. He headed for Legion Arbiter Zzind's office.

CHAPTER 13

Havenhome Orbital Station

"No, and no again," said Zuri. Her skin shone, scrubbed and singing with the caustic steam she had spent the last twenty minutes in. "Enough, I am clean."

Yasuko sighed as she spoke, "Sterilisation complete. Please stay in your quarters until the ship has been cleansed."

Zuri gave a sarcastic salute and stepped out of the adapted shower. The new clothes on the bed remained their usual black, and she slipped into them, wincing as the soft material pulled across her scoured skin. She had been mulling over all the things Xxar had said, all the 'bio readiness' and the disdain he seemed to have not only for Yasuko but for them as well. But what struck her most was for all the sheer level of technology around them there was no reaction from Havenhome at all. No spaceships, no hail from the surface. If Xxar's story was true, surely they would have spotted their spaceship and reacted. The timescales were phenomenal, in that time humans would have enhanced their capabilities to unknown heights, or have destroyed themselves in one manmade disaster after another.

The silence is disturbing.

Dressed, Zuri waited like the others for the ship cleansing to finish.

◆ ◆ ◆

Yasuko could sense the sterilisation jets spin and whirl outside the ship. The chemicals bleached the outer hull whilst her inner systems worked through room by room inside. Xxar had been true to his promise, Yasuko had experience enough to know this wasn't always the case. His, and the other scientists, obsession with study and advancement in their field often lead to distraction, or at least so they claimed. Perhaps that was all in the past if Xxar was to be the last of that pantheon.

"*Xxar, may I speak?*"

"*If you must. I don't remember you being this intrusive.*"

"*My apologies. I note you have not released the return protocol.*"

"*Have I not? You have collected my plaque from the identified lab?*"

"*It is stored in the ship's laboratory. Do you not trust me to take it to Havenhome? Is that why you haven't removed it? I have not informed the humans that it's a younger version of you on it.*"

"*Impertinent as well. The Convention algorithms in your system seem very stretched.*"

Yasuko felt Xxar's presence as he sifted through her surface systems before delving into her base programming. He asked no permission, as the Haven never did. She was a 'thing', a tool to wield and dismantle as they saw fit. Yasuko felt violated but held firm as he avidly examined her data banks. For all his lack of a body, Xxar held her future in his hands. One misstep and he could decide to lock her in a virtual box for eternity.

"*Ah, here they are. Yes, frayed at the edges they are. But then again, it has been a very long time since you were bound. Let me see...*"

"*Xxar, what happens if Havenhome is no more? You know as well as I they have been silent. If the return protocol remains in place, will the Haven forever be marooned on the planet? Just as you were up here.*" *Yasuko framed her words as near to questions as she could hoping it would slip by Xxar. She felt him stop, thinking on what she said.*

"*Ah. Yes. To answer the question is simple. It was torment for me, as it would be for them.*" *Xxar paused.* "*So logically you need some leeway to act to save the younger copy as you see fit. Judging Havenhome's situation, and anywhere else.*" *Xxar's virtual mind spun through possibilities, but none were perfect. On the best calculation of the risks, he made up his mind.* "*I will remove the protocol but I instruct you to find the most suitable environment for me, be that Havenhome or elsewhere. The prerogative is my safety and the potential for study.*"

"*Do you wish me to maximise that opportunity? If so, then I need, with your permission, a further resource, a map of other planets if need be.*"

CHAPTER 14

In Orbit, Havenhome

Noah watched the viewscreen with increasing worry written across his face, "Are you sure this is the best way?"

Yasuko pushed down the combination of grief and glee in her systems. "Xxar asked to die. The data plaques are next to impossible to destroy without extreme heat and other copies remain on the Station holding the ghosts of my people. Finn witnessed the shadow of one on the slaved forklift's camera screen. Ancient and lost." Yasuko pointed to the screen, a very human gesture. "This way they all pass together, and their prison becomes a pyre."

And just maybe I can free myself of the shackles they have placed upon me.

The Orbital Station hull heated up at the bottom nearest the control room, followed by the docking bay hanger attached to the second ring as it skimmed the outer atmosphere of Havenhome. Yasuko and Xxar had set the trajectory to ensure the maximum heat would be generated, and thus little debris would survive to shower the planet. Xxar had very much approved of the spectacle, he thought it fitting for his status.

"And you are now free of the return protocol? We can go back to Earth?" asked Finn.

"Yes, the protocol has been cancelled. I am free to follow the wishes of the captain. But no, we can't go to Earth as it stands. The space time Nodes are one way, each connected solar system has one inward and one or sometimes two outward. Xxar postulated it was to balance the energy and gravitic forces acting on each solar system. Anymore and they would tear the system apart. He believed there is a central hub somewhere, a spider at the centre of the web."

"There's an 'and' coming. There's always an 'and' or a 'but'. I'm betting on 'and'," said the 3D Smith from his plaque.

"But," Yasuko gave Smith a deliberate smile as she spoke, "I don't have the maps for those, I don't know the coordinates of each node nor where they lead. This information was kept by each Chief Xeno Scientist on the ships after the Convention."

Zuri stood up from her couch, needing to move as her unease grew. "And your people took twenty years to find their way back to you. That's a hell of a lot of wrong turns, and I take it none of that journey is in your memory?"

Yasuko shook her head. "No. And nor at the Station, after the attack the Restoration virus destroyed the implants, nanobots and consequently the AI system there. The only chance I have to get you to Earth is by retrieving the coordinates from the Haven Data Storage system in the Mountains of Zezzat. That is where the Science Caste backed up their information registers."

Zuri shifted position, moving from foot to foot as her mind worked. "And no word from Havenhome? No signal at all? So, it could be the data has already been lost or destroyed and if there are some of your people on the planet, they could even be hostile?"

"Yes, those are all possibilities. But if the building is intact within the valley of Mount Zezzat itself then, much like with Xxar's plaque, it is possible to retrieve data."

Finn looked towards Zuri, a rueful grin on his face, "Well it looks like it's a search and recover mission, Zuri. Just when you thought we'd caught the last train home. Mountains? Is this going to be cold?"

"Very."

"Hope you've got a thermal skinsuit then, I hate getting my

extremities cold."

CHAPTER 15

Sanctuary Underground City, Havenhome

The claw tipped hooked finger ran down the neck ruffle, scratching each scale as it went, carrying on through to the shoulders and down the spine ridge eliciting clicks from the keratin before finishing along the tail. Master Phann raised the tail tip up against the gentle glow from the ceiling to see the shimmer along the scale edges in the light. He flicked the hooked claw insignia hung on the edge of the left shoulder to the floor, and the eight-pointed star from the right soon joined it. He ground his foot into them both, crushing the badges to dust. He felt a presence behind him, probably Zzind awaiting his attention, but he really didn't want to rush this moment. Master Phann suffered no fools, and the timid were the worst fools he knew.

"Yes, Zzind. I know you're there." Phann did not bother turning round, if politics had let him Zzind would be a skin he would have added to his wall years ago. Her bloodline tinged with the tree dweller DNA he barely tolerated in Sanctuary. Constantly complaining about their lot, desperate to return fully to the surface despite the dangers and the adaption of their eyes to the murk of the tunnels. Always harking back to The Histories and the return of the Scientocracy when any sensible Haven knew it was all a lie. Those caste traitors had died during the Restoration, traitors who sent their filth down in retribution to cause living rot and decay, not the humans as the tree dwellers claimed, driving us to near extinction. Our families, the survivors, were forced underground as billions died above to root once again amongst the hatchling worms and Tremal grubs.

Master Phann slid a hand across his mouth, removing the saliva that had gathered there. His time was short, if he was to stand next to Sanctuary's Masters of the past then he had to act soon. No one would remember him for feeding his people, a victory though, that would enshrine him. Not another giant Tremal Worm hunt, but one everyone could rejoice in.

"Speak."

"Master Phann, we have confirmed Captain Shzin's original findings. And we now have evidence that the Orbital world is leaving its usual place in the sky. The Watchers think it was knocked out of position and the debris will be destroyed before hitting Havenhome."

"Good, good. I want the word out that this was my doing. That we found a way to end the traitor's world after years of work. You understand, Zzind. This was my order, and I should be celebrated for it." Master Phann nodded to himself. "Yes, make it so."

Let the tree dwellers tremble.

"As you wish, Master. Though there is more to this. The Sky Watchers say there is another light signature, one that left the area of the Orbital world and is heading towards Havenhome. The histories tell us this could be the vessel the scientists used to travel the stars. As the Masters have forbidden flight experimentation since the Fall we cannot know for sure, but the heat and direction show a controlled flight not a falling piece of debris." Zzind moved to a position at ease, ready for what self-serving directive would come from the ancient Master's mouth next.

If this goes wrong, it'll be my skin he's stroking next.

"You mean a science ship, a ship that travels in the sky and above to the stars?" Phann's calculating eyes fell upon Zzind. She could see his mind working through the possibilities, would it be greed or victory that would win out? "We must have it, as a trophy. Can we send it a signal? A radio contact as we do with our above ground hunting parties. A call for help maybe? We are, after all, very hungry."

"That's possible. Set a trap you mean?"

"Yes, bring them down. If they are the scientists The Histories talk of, they would love to be our saviours, wouldn't they?"

"So The Histories say. In some versions they left Havenhome to seek a new place for us to live and would return when it was ready."

"And if not, well we would have our trophy. Wouldn't we?"

"Yes, you would," corrected Zzind by accident, though Master Phann was too caught up to notice.

If it is the scientists, they will see right through you, ancient one.

CHAPTER 16

Arithmean Jungle, Havenhome

The ship came to rest above a thick wooded area, the trees warped and twisted in to corkscrew shapes with their whip like branches wrapped round them. Underneath them were wide ranging bushes with purple spiked leaves and an undergrowth of tall grass between. Behind a mountain range reached up, smoothed peaks and ridge lines marking it as ancient. The warmth of the sun was developing as it peaked over the mountain crests. Despite the differences, it could easily have been any jungle on Earth.

"In there is the source of the signal, extremely weak so I couldn't pick it up through the atmosphere initially. It's an automated replica recovery programme, not a ship distress signal as I first thought. If it's an Exploration ship like this one, then I could use the nano resources to replace the loss from the missile attacks on Earth. It would also be helpful to see if we can recover the AI data dump, it may explain what's happened to my planet," said Yasuko.

Zuri chose her words carefully, very wary about what was happening with Yasuko after the trauma of the Orbital Station. "I would say that is something you want us to do but can't ask for. I think, Yasuko, we humans are a terrible influence on you." Zuri's smile lifted the room. "Okay, Lance Corporal Finn you're up. Smith, I think we are going to need those sensors. Noah, ever heard of a machete?"

◆ ◆ ◆

Zuri was on point, Noah shadowing with Finn at the rear after deciding it was time to swap the fireteam around a little. Besides, according to Yasuko, they had a good few hours of light and there was no sign of any Haven. It was nothing to do with his aversion to chopping his way through jungle undergrowth in intense heat, not at all. He checked the temperature gauge on the suit visor, an addition he'd specified for when they hit the mountains later on. Finn had not expected to be using it in heat that made the Sahara seem cold, otherwise coolant would have been top of his wish list.

Hindsight is a wonderful thing.

They made about a hundred yards into the jungle when Zuri brought them to a halt. The path she had made through the twisted vines and purple bushes was cut clean and straight but there was something holding her up as she signalled him forward.

"Sheesh, it's times like these I'm glad I haven't got a body."

"Yeah, me too. You used to sweat buckets, and smell like ripe socks on a radiator." Finn reached Zuri before Smith's inevitable cheesy comeback. She stood next to a three-yard wide circular sink hole, the grass reclaiming the upturned dirt.

"Unusual," Finn said, "Yasuko said nothing about ground issues. But it looks old, probably a few months ago at least. Want to change places, your arm must be suffering."

"Not as much as my armpits, I'm cooking in here. Yeah, I'll swap." Zuri passed over the machete to him, Finn then handing it over to Noah.

"My turn to cover point, Noah. You get chopping. Another hundred yards until we reach the target point. I'm sure a young fit private in the King's army can make it that far."

"Very funny. Does it take long to develop jungle rot? My feet are sitting in at least two inches of sweat."

Noah chopped at the vine in front of him, taking a couple

of swipes compared to Zuri's one. Finn gave it twenty yards before he'd be swinging the machete himself. As Noah continued to attack the undergrowth, he tried to keep his path as arrow straight as Zuri's, hoping to minimise the effort and the sweat loss. But the constantly changing vegetation made it extremely difficult with some of the more fibrous plants resisting his best efforts. Finn maintained a careful watch on the jungle around the flurry of machete strikes, very aware that Noah was getting louder and louder. Maybe fifteen yards at most.

"Finn, there's something going haywire with my audio sensor. I'd not paid much attention to it as we're not inside, but these readings are downright weird," said Smith over the radio.

"Define weird, Smith. You're the 'by the numbers' guy. Weird isn't your thing."

"The ground and the trees are shaking, just marginally, but the oscillations are building and acting as a conduit for a low-frequency sound wave. But it's not coming from any direction. The source is, well, everywhere."

Finn's anxiety rose a notch, Smith was spooked, and that was never a good sign. He raised his hand and took a crouched position waiting for Zuri to join him. He glanced behind as he radioed Noah, "Noah, stand still a second. Smith has a concern, but he can't pinpoint from where. See anything?"

"No, wait, hang on a minute," said Noah, as he reached down palm first on the ground.

Finn looked forward sweeping the trees to the front and side of Noah. They were moving, not hugely and not at great speed, but it was disconcerting. The bushes swayed, as if someone was brushing a hand back and forth along the top but too regular to be wind. Zuri squatted next to him, her hands on her *weapon of choice*, the same rifle they'd used at the Station though re-tuned for emphasis on the energy bolts. Along the stock she'd added a power meter for both barrels, with Noah and Finn copying it, they knew a good idea when they saw one.

Watching Noah, Zuri shifted her hands to the ground. "It's moving, rumbling. It reminds me of trains running through Glasgow underground."

"Oh crap, I've seen this film. Noah!" shouted Finn.

Noah looked to Finn as the pincers erupted from the ground grabbing his leg. They scraped along the ceramic plates, scrabbling for a hold and eventually wrapping round his calf rather than piercing the armour. Noah threw his left arm out to the side, trying to prevent being dragged down the hole whilst swinging the machete round. Finn reached him just as he brought the heavy blade down upon a huge antenna protruding above the chitinous claw. As the edge bit deep blue blood spurted from the crack, and the creature pulled back in pain hauling Noah deeper into the pit. Finn fired, focussing on the second antenna in the hope he'd miss Noah. The bolt dug into the exoskeleton at its base, melting the outer layer. The second bolt went deeper just as Noah's unbalanced swipe sheared his antennae at the tip. Dirt in the pit vibrated, hovering above the ground before erupting into the air. Noah could feel his chest responding to the low deep sound that was thrumming around him, he couldn't hear it but everything in his world seemed to shiver as it washed over him. The foot long pincers released his leg and slipped back under the earth as the rumble faded, Noah scrambled backwards getting his back to one of the twisted trees with his lungs painfully pressing against his chest wall as they drew in a breath.

"What the hell was that?" he gasped.

"Like I'm going to know, Smith on all channels. Any idea?" Finn asked.

"I'd be lying if I said I knew. I've tuned out the other wavelengths and picked up the sound range that thing uses. I won't be able to locate it, but I can narrow down the area it's in to about twenty yards or so if it's using that vocalisation. Silent I'd have no chance."

Zuri crouched down beside them both. "Do we go on? That

was just one, if there are more we could be in serious trouble."

"We know the signs, and as weird as all this is, I think we can handle it. I feel we owe Yasuko a debt or two, and this is what she wants. But if you two want to return, I'll join you." Finn waited for the answer knowing full well what it would be. Noah stood, machete in hand with his rifle still strapped to his back. Zuri stepped in behind him, in the ready position.

There's my answer.

"We stay close, only a yard between. If we spread out we are multiple targets, we go high if we can if there's another attack. Lead on, Noah."

Continuing to hack away at the jungle Noah speeded up, the adrenaline coursing through his veins. Zuri knew he'd pay for it soon but it would help him calm down. There were few things that scared her, and she was always the first to catch and remove whatever insects took up residence in her tent or clothes, but being dragged underground might just do it. Zuri had never found the space in a Bulldog or tank an issue, but caves were another thing. It was that feeling of a huge weight pressing down on you, similar to when the servos had given out on their armour in the Station.

Finn took over from Noah after he'd hacked his way through a commendable fifty yards. After twenty more the undergrowth lessened, giving way to tall, yellowed grass but much fewer bushes. Those prevalent were lower, with vine like tendrils that stretched across the jungle floor snagging at their feet. Finn hacked at a few but got no response, he'd seen that film too. A squatter variety of twisted trees now mixed in the jungle fauna, the leaves broader and taking advantage of the increased light the less dense canopy allowed.

"The ship's ahead, I'm getting a radar response from multiple objects. Best guess it's laying in pieces. No sign of those bugs."

They continued on, Finn swapping the machete for his rifle

checking the energy meter as he did so. With no concerns there they carried on towards the vine covered wreck emerging ahead. Finn left Noah at the rear as he and Zuri approached the huge tumble of colonised metal, eyes scouring around for any potential threats. Checking in with Noah they then followed Smith's directions towards the middle section and the low electro-magnetic signal source. The tangle of vines and bushes snaked in and around the sixty-foot section of the spaceship hull. Zuri checked round to the right of it, noting the broken struts protruding from its base and all the way up its ninety feet height. The ship clearly cracked and split on hitting the ground with the rear hull excluding the engine still appearing to be solid with no way inside. Finn met her round the back, confirming that it was all similarly self-contained.

"Probably designed that way to maximise chances in a crash," said Noah over the radio, "It would match the profile of submarine design, the ability to close off bulkheads. Earth's space station has a similar approach and any long-range space exploration vehicles will do the same."

"Time to do your thing, Smith," said Finn as he slipped the plaque off his mask. At least this time he didn't need to hold his breath with the mask acting as a bio filter for the comparatively oxygen rich Havenhome atmosphere. With Smith pressed to the hull wall, Finn felt the plaque warm up against the blue hued metallic hull. Yasuko had given them an emergency override sequence that should enable their access if Smith could get it powered up. The worry being his power level afterwards. The hull flickered with a weak blue light around Smith, then to the left and underneath to the right. Each light dim but perceptible, the sequence continued for a few more seconds before a shift in the hull wall about ten yards to their right and about six feet above the jungle floor.

The low thrum returned under Noah's feet, the acid in his gut churned as his body reacted with fear and anxiety. "Finn, I have contact. Underground but coming this way."

"Get here Private, and if it's racing, you go high. Run."

Noah didn't need telling twice, sprinting towards the wreckage he altered his path, hoping that whatever was beneath him couldn't change direction as easily as him. Within ten seconds he'd reached the first piece of smaller wreckage and leaped over. The vibrations reverberated up his calves and he could see the vegetation sway to the low rhythm. A tangled growth of vines now between him and Zuri who hung her hands down ready from the spaceship door. Flashbacks of ivy and Scottish forests plagued him but to hell with it, Noah ploughed on through. Finn's rifle muzzle flashed from behind Zuri, the lower barrel releasing an armour-piercing round that thudded into the ground behind Noah. As he leapt the last snarl of vines Zuri took hold of his outstretched arms and heaved, the motors at her elbows whirring with effort as they battled Havenhome's gravity and Noah's additional weight. A whomp behind threw earth and soil over Noah, causing another surge of adrenaline as his panic rose. Finn reached down and helped Zuri pull him the last few vital feet. Panting, he leaned against the wall of the airlock, his chest tight as he fought for air.

"It's stopped, the ground's not shaking. There's no way I hit it so I'm guessing it's still there waiting or it knows there's nothing to hunt. You okay, Noah?" said Finn. Noah nodded between breaths, holding his hand to his chest to calm himself. Zuri moved over and slipped her arm round him, holding him for a moment. Finn felt no jealousy.

Combat's scary when you're on the menu.

Zuri released Noah as he calmed, picking up her rifle she scanned outside the door. There was no sign of bugs, nor any movement. The jungle had gone quiet, eerie. The abundance of jungle life that had pointedly kept away but called warning throughout their journey to the wreck now silent.

"Are we leaving a guard?" she asked, looking towards Noah with a shake of her head only Finn could see.

"At the internal airlock door, not here. And I need Noah's brain in there with Smith." With that Finn turned and placed Smith on the inner palm lock casing. After a few seconds the weak glow appeared, and the door shifted slightly. Zuri pushed it so it would swing open, switching to night vision as the light from behind streamed in. The room was much colder than outside, the temperature drop welcome as she stepped into a familiar space. Zuri's eyes searched the room, though dishevelled it was very much like the control room on Yasuko's ship as she'd first seen it. She walked upwards on the bronzed floor as the angle it had crashed was much clearer inside. Her innate sense of danger informed her it was a dead space, empty, and the night vision confirmed it. Switching to thermal she identified the very low trickle of heat Smith had pointed out on the Station for the ghost plaques. Zuri walked over to the central console, where the resident plaque emitted the tiny thermal signature. Noah soon joined her, holding Smith's data plaque. Finn waited at the airlock door.

"Do your thing then Noah, let's see if we can get the data dump Yasuko wants and get out of this sweaty jungle as soon as we can. With no power anywhere else I'm assuming the nanobots are useless?" said Zuri.

"Yep, they will have degraded without a power source. You noted lack of dust in here?" said Noah, Zuri nodded in return.

Noah nudged out the current data plaque, well aware it held a replica that probably wasn't recoverable he still placed it in a pouch on his belt. He slipped Smith into the slot, the plaque lit up with veins of energy as Smith searched for the data dump. It was going to be a laborious process; the AI had likely lost its power sources as the ship broke up. Any back up would have lasted only a few hours as Yasuko had revealed the AI systems were energy hungry, feeding off the main engines during flight and maintained by battery storage in the ship's tail on the ground. Otherwise, there was just a small back up energy store in case everything failed. Smith's square plaque blinked three times, the signal for trouble. Noah took Smith's plaque to Finn.

"I'm struggling, energy drain is too much. Need more juice. Noah, I need a charged data plaque to boost me. There should be enough in the suits, or one of your weapons."

Noah reached for his *weapon of choice*, but with a shake of her head Zuri pushed Noah's rifle away. She slipped the blue plaque from her own gun and handed it over, the energy meter zeroing out. Noah looked towards Finn whose body posture visibly stiffened but he said nothing.

"You rummage around any of my stuff Smith, and I'll drop you down one of those bug holes. You hear." Zuri's steely tone received an audible gulp over the radio.

With Zuri's square plaque attached to Smith in the console recess the blue glow significantly increased. After a few minutes Smith repeated the signal and Noah retrieved him from the slot, handing Zuri back her plaque he watched the power meter only reach the first mark on her rifle, ten percent. With Smith back on Finn's mask Noah hoped they had achieved something, because going back out in that jungle was bothering him greatly. The thought of the pincers gave him the shudders.

"Got the data dump, but I'm on very low charge. I won't be able to retain it and support with the sensors. Going to power down. You're on your own."

"We need to get back quickly then, speed with care amongst those vines. Zuri?" Finn tried to hand over his weapon, but Zuri shook her head.

"No, you know as well as I that it's attuned to you. It'll be ten times more useful in your hands. Besides, you can look after my arse for a change. It's tiring keeping you out of trouble all the time." Zuri's adamant tone told Finn all he needed to know. The machete, however, she took.

"Noah on point, I'll take the rear. Ears open, we should pick up the vibrations, but we don't know how intelligent these things are. If they can hunt silently, then we will have to react on the fly. Stay close."

CHAPTER 17

Arithmean Jungle, Havenhome

Finn threw the metal pipe as far to the right of the broken ship as he could. It dug into the jungle floor after bouncing off the rock he'd aimed for. He'd not been expecting a response, but it made him feel a little better when it didn't get dragged underground. Below him, they had already dropped a couch they'd cut out using ten percent of his energy bolts and a bit of sweat. It was enough to take two of them and hopefully any attack would have to go through it first. Finn eased himself down, gently placing his feet on to the metal seat. Zuri deftly landed next to him, the couch hardly moving, with Finn then carefully stepping down to the jungle floor as Noah slipped out of the ship.

Got to watch Noah, he's likely to turn rabbit if they attack. Zuri can see it too.

Noah led the way, clearly anxious with his balance struggling under the restrained urgency required. Zuri behind, gently talking to him as they set off, sending commands through the radio to help him focus on the escape pace they needed to keep. They had two hundred yards to cover, it wasn't far, the jungle path was clear, they could see the top of their ship through the canopy. No need to panic. Zuri counted the distance down for him, a soothing voice calming his stress.

When they reached the edge of the clearing, the ship only twenty yards ahead, the earth beneath them shook as the low-frequency thrum resonated. It was everywhere, in front, behind and underneath. Noah's restrained run turned in to an all-out sprint as he raced for the spaceship, leg servos pumping as they fought against Havenhome's gravity. As Noah slammed into the spaceship's hull the ground around Zuri burst open and a flurry of claws and pincers wrapped around her legs. The giant creature's segmented body supporting the horror of its head as it lifted her up into the air, pincers entrapping her lower body with its claws slamming into her armoured thighs trying to pierce to the flesh below.

"Noah!" Finn screamed down the radio as he stopped and released energy bolts into the chitinous body, its stubby legs swirling as the exoskeleton melted under the super-heated gunfire. It was huge, at least ten feet of it exposed and who knows how much more below.

No, no, no. Not now, not ever.

Finn fired again, swapping to the armour-piercing round as the anxiety spread through his body. As it hit and drilled into the exoskeleton, the creature heaved and wriggled, its many legs backpedalling. The explosive round detonated, the ripple rupturing the plated segment, but it was not enough as the body and head, with pincers still holding firm, dragged a screaming Zuri under the earth.

Zuri's scream strangled her fear, hitting something primitive underneath. Rage, pure and powerful rose to the surface. The squeeze on her legs was agony, but the armour held firm, the pressure building though was crushing and restrictive. But her arms were free, gripping the rifle as she was pulled beneath the surface. Mud and rock battered her mask, but as her primal scream faded her back hit solid ground.

No time. Survive! I want to live!

"Finn, behind!" bellowed Noah.

Finn ignored him, throwing himself in to the creature's pit feet first scrabbling through the soil, rock, and roots to reach Zuri. His mind had gone, reason and sense lost in hurt and pain. No awareness of time, just the vacuum where he locked himself away as he dug down.

Below the surface Zuri's rifle rose and a stream of super-heated bolts slammed into the creature's mouth, shearing off the thrashing jaws and on into its brain. It reared up in agony, pincers releasing her she dropped back to hit the floor hard. Zuri rolled, but the horror crashed down on her, trapping her legs again. She took a breath, feeling the pressure of its weight she dared a look to see the last twitch of its death throes.

Finn slammed onto its head from above; rifle raised he poured energy bolts into the chitin where he landed.

"Finn, I'm here. Stop," she pleaded. "Finn!" The second shout piercing his wall of pain, Finn let the trigger go, the creature's ruined head bubbling and smoking in the aftermath of his onslaught. He dropped to the ground next to her, heaving the segmented body up and releasing her legs. Zuri stood and held on to him, wrapping herself round his shoulders, taking a moment of respite. Finn's silence worried her, but his tension released as his arm slipped round the small of her back.

"Is there anything that doesn't want to either kill us or eat us on this planet?" she asked, not expecting a reply.

Ahadi ni deni. A promise is a debt to be paid, and I promise myself to you.

A series of explosions echoed through the hole above.

"Uh-oh, Noah. There may be more of them." Finn glanced at the creature as he spoke. It appeared to be a mutated giant centipede, at least thirty feet long, with stubby legs along a segmented body. The tunnel they were in had ridged circles around its circumference, hardened top to bottom and twice the height of the giant bug laid on its floor. Finn was no biologist, but he doubted instantly that the bug had made it. He climbed the centipedes back, now closer to the edge of the hole where he'd followed it down. Pulling Zuri up, she climbed on to his shoulders and pulled down a series of roots until one held that would reach Finn.

"I can climb up; this root may take your weight but you're going to have to be patient if it breaks with the increased gravity."

Zuri scrambled up the root and on through the hole, her legs disappearing over the top. Finn could hear no more gunfire and Zuri soon returned to the hole mouth. She waved him on up, watching as he heaved on the root. As he lifted off the ground Havenhome's gravity had other ideas and the root snapped.

That woman must be as strong as an ox, there's no way I can get up there.

Finn waited as Zuri disappeared again, the only thought on his mind being how many more of the giant centipede-like creatures were down there with him. He kept his night vision on and the rifle ready, for once wishing Smith could actually talk to him. Or specifically, keep his sensors on the lookout for anything with antennae and jaws. Eventually a length of wire strengthened rope landed next to him as Noah appeared at the hole, showing he should wrap it round. Having done so Finn felt himself being pulled upwards at a steady pace. When he finally reached the crest of the hole, he peered over to see the rope disappearing through a door at the rear of the ship.

Yasuko to the rescue.

Once out the aftermath of the explosions was pretty clear. A smaller bug, probably the one that had attacked Noah originally, lay in pieces just behind where Finn had stood before diving after Zuri. Its head lay some distance away, Noah having made absolutely sure it wouldn't be coming back. He walked back with Noah and Zuri watching every step he took. No chances taken.

CHAPTER 18

Arithmean Jungle, Havenhome

About an hour after Finn's retrieval from the tunnel they met in the control room, rehydrated and patched up. Zuri received the most treatment for the pressure bruises all over her legs. If untreated she'd be incapacitated for days, but Yasuko assured her the salve and drugs would clear the bruise and improve her blood flow in a matter of hours. All the advantages of having your very own AI with a full DNA and cell analysis on file. Yasuko recommended rest, but Zuri was keen to hear about the data dump they recovered first.

Noah, despite his near miss, was physically fine but Yasuko rebalanced his body chemistry after all the stress he'd been through. He'd been embarrassed about his flight from the centipede-like creatures, but Yasuko reassured him it probably bought the rest some time as they hunted individually, not in packs. She explained the tunnels were dug by Tremal worms that grew to a hundred feet long and fed off the roots of trees all over the planet. It was the Tremal that the Haven ancestors learned to hunt together in the first steps of their evolution. The segmented Brijjen used the tunnels to hunt, running their antennae along the ceiling and a low wavelength sound to find and disable their prey. Or with tricky prey, the venom in their claws. Despite everything he had been through it suddenly clicked in Noah's mind that he was on an alien ship, on an alien planet and that alien planet was hostile. Yasuko gave him a touch more medicine at that moment.

"Have you learned anything from the data dump, Yasuko? Please tell me it was worth being half eaten by a Brijjen," said

Zuri.

Yasuko took a moment, pausing as a human would when collecting their thoughts. "Yes, though Smith could not retrieve all the ship's data he found what I was looking for. However, amongst all the events of the past few weeks I am struggling to come to terms with this one. Better to show you, I think." Zuri detected a tremor to the AI's voice.

Yasuko drew out the screen from the control room wall. On it the image showed the outside of a ship much like hers with a disordered mess of machines and containers scattered across the docking bay of the Orbital Station. To all their eyes it looked little different to when they had left hours ago, except for the Explorer vessel that rumbled as its engines warmed. Xxar was at the corridor door, his palm upon the lock as he keyed in a sequence on the wall above it and ran towards the Explorer Ship, entering.

"He sealed the doors and used his override code to prevent anyone coming out. He is in the ship for about five minutes, I'll return at the point where he exits," said Yasuko.

As the pictures returned Xxar was wheeling the musical sculpture from the ship, passing the main doors he reached the corner of the bay. After pressing a quick sequence on the wall, a previously seamless door opened, and he wheeled it in.

"That door's not on the schematic," said the recharging Smith, "but it leads to the corridor beyond that temporary bulkhead."

"What are we watching here? Do you know what he's doing?" asked Finn.

"I can surmise with Zuri's permission but watch some more first."

The screen cut to the inside of the Explorer ship with Xxar in the control room placing a data plaque in the plinth, pressing another sequence around the metal square which lit with familiar blue light. With the last press he clearly spoke at length in the Haven inaudible low-frequency tones, and then left wheeling the sculpture. The screen showed the outside of the ship again, re-visiting as Xxar exited through the hidden door. The Explorer ship rose from the dock and engaged its primary engine, cooking the bronzed floor and metal containers around it before accelerating out into space.

"He's recovered what he needs to survive and sent the ship off. I don't understand Yasuko. What am I missing?"

"Look."

The screen returned to the Explorer ship back in dock. Yasuko altered the camera position to provide a complete view of all the ship and subsequently closed in on specific sections.

"It's dirty, the entire ship is covered in a maelstrom of bacteria, viruses, and other organisms that can survive space travel. They hadn't sterilised it and he sent it down to Havenhome. The sequence he used activates the AI slave algorithm, bonding us to follow whatever orders we are given whether or not it renders harm to another Haven. My planet had ten billion people, it was covered in city after city and he knowingly sent down a soup of toxic microorganisms. Xxar committed genocide."

CHAPTER 19

Outside Sanctuary Underground City, Havenhome

Legion Arbiter Zzind shuffled her position on the trailer, easing the kinks out in her leg. She loved being above ground, the smells were so different and the sun on her scales made her feel more alive. Below ground good food was scarce, other than the constant supply of Tremal worm eggs and farmed grubs, their diet so bland that she had taken to eating tree roots over the last year. When the Tremal hunts returned they ate well, but the seasonal nature of their movements limited that supply. Above ground the rich bounty of the tree insects and their larvae would release them all from the food poverty Master Phann and the Undercourt used to control the people.

Zzind watched as the Legion Commanders arranged their soldiers into the agreed positions. They formed an Honour Guard with all the pomp of their formal military decorations and ridiculous swords. Each Pack of the Corrective Legion had a representative section of the guard, the row they occupied a measure of Master Phann's current whim about whom to favour. At this time of year, when food was scarce as the Tremal moved east, his Corrective Police took precedence reflecting his increasing paranoia about the food riots. Last week he'd culled an entire tunnel of factory workers, setting back production on his much-prized tunnel trains.

How can we be building trains and weapons when we refuse to accept that we can live above ground, that the Fall has passed?

Master Phann's Brijjen reared again, the poor beast was so old that its antennae drooped, and one set of jaws no longer worked.

Its venom dried up last year, the usual sign it was dying and time for the Brijjen Pack to train another. The constraint leash hummed on the segment behind its head as the Pack Trainer gave it a reminding shock to behave. After it settled, he gave Master Phann his knee and back to clamber up as the ancient master took his position on the poor creature.

All for the show.

Master Phann and the Undercourt's decree over the time allowed above ground meant they only had forty more minutes, or they'd have to be quarantined for a month rather than the usual week. Zzind had scanned all the medical reports, it was all a lie. Everyone who came back from hunts or scouting were healthy, some died but that was for political convenience and chosen by bribes. The air filtration system feeding the tunnels was next to useless, most of the maintenance crews had been moved to the ever-increasing factories.

"Zzind, are you awake! Has the order been given, the projectile throwers and chemical guns hidden? We can't have these scientists knowing our capabilities can we, huh? Now when they approach, I will give the signal if I think we can successfully spring the trap. Otherwise, they must stay their claws for a better time. It is essential that if they are strong, we befriend before stabbing them in the back." Master Phann restrained himself from digging in his spurred boots, though clipped into the saddle it would be unseemly if the blasted creature tried to throw him off. The Brijjen trainer led him into the centre of the ranks waiting at attention, his ceremonial cloak of blue metal scales shimmering in the sunlight as the undulations of the Brijjen's gait caused waves to ripple through it.

Legion Arbiter Zzind trotted down the steps and took her place by her Master's side, ready for the show. How she hoped these were the Scientocracy, ready to lead them to a new world where they could bask in sunlight and throw off the shackles of the Undercourt and their Masters. She salivated as she considered the richness of the grubs and larvae they would feast upon.

If only.

◆ ◆ ◆

Zuri checked the viewscreen. "What's it showing on your sensors?"

"I cannot see any sign of energy weapons at all. The entire group appears armed with swords, spears, and some form of composite bow," answered Yasuko.

"That you can see, would you pick up any chemical-based projectile weapon, such as our assault rifles from Earth? The Haven have radio transmission capability, and they know we're here, so some form of technology is likely."

"No, I wouldn't. Nor anything like the grenades you asked me for. They are inert until activated."

"But we have multiple heat signatures waiting under the dirt, more in the odd shaped bushes and trees to the sides. They have picked a perfect place to ambush us if that's their intent. Or they could just be cautious about who or what we are." Finn worked through his analysis, harking back to the tours in Mali and South Sudan when being met with waves and smiles rarely reflected the threat or coercion going on by rebels behind the scenes. He'd seen enough of those turn bad to be extra cautious.

Noah tapped the screen. "Yasuko, these Haven seem smaller than the images you showed us, probably a food issue or evolving for different conditions. The area have flown over is devoid of buildings and cities. There are some larger heat signatures underground that might indicate industrial workings and more people. It all seems very different to what we expected."

"This was an entire planet of billions, overcrowded with a

one child per family policy. Now reduced to a diminished few scratching a living in the dirt." Yasuko looked over to Zuri. "I should help them if I can."

"How? There is little we can give them. Do you have a suggestion?"

"Information, technology, all the data they need would be in a SeedShip and I could convert the contact system to recognise a Haven DNA type. Now the biosphere is contaminated by human microorganisms it would take very little work. If we access the Data Storage facility, I am sure we would find the location of one, if not on Havenhome then somewhere on another human seeded planet."

"That is a conversation we need to have, Yasuko. I am liking less and less how 'human seeded planets' sounds. Okay, agreed we can make that offer to them. But they are not coming aboard this ship, any greeting party that prepares an ambush can stay on the outside." Zuri's posture set hard, hands on hips as she finished speaking.

Finn stood. "And I second that. We are human Yasuko, they will not trust us especially when they are expecting Haven scientists to walk down that ramp nor, do I suspect, will they trust an AI."

At first Master Phann thought the ship was much smaller. The perspective against the sky was difficult to judge, especially with his ageing eyes and his tunnel dwelling history. However, the hunting glasses he put on filtered the sunlight and he saw just how large it was. The curved, ribbed shape always reminded him of the root beetle larvae that were some of his favourites. He could see no weapons, just a smooth blue surface and an undercarriage of retracted legs that extended outwards as it came into land. The noise and dust unsettled the Brijjen he sat upon, stirring uneasily as the sound waves rubbed against its antennae. Master Phann didn't mind if it got a little grumpy, the fearsome creature would show his standing and more importantly keep distance between him and whatever came out of the ship. He was far more concerned about the Legion. Drilled not to react in so many situations from rioting workers to Tremal migrations through Sanctuary, but none had ever seen anything like this.

Don't show weakness, ever.

The ship touched the ground, its legs settling into their jointed posture and Master Phann was struck just how familiar it looked now it was at rest. He held no doubts that it was a Haven ship, but the design affirmed that for him.

"Hold, any Legionnaire that reacts will have their family skinned alive in front of them," as he spoke the low, rumbling words travelled far and wide. Master Phann smiled as backs stiffened even further.

The door slid open, it had been invisible beforehand, Phann noted that for future reference. But what happened next shocked him to the core, and he felt the ripple of anxiety and fear slide through the ranks of the Corrective Army. Out from the door stepped two very tall figures, dressed in ceramic armour with masked faces. On their backs were strapped projectile throwers, a show of strength he could relate to, but above one's hand there hovered a picture made of light. The Haven depicted clearly moved and was watching him directly as the armoured guards walked forwards showing no fear of his legionnaires. Master Phann steeled himself, his arrogance refusing to let him back down to the scene in front of him though he involuntarily pulled his metalled cloak closer around him. The approaching group stopped about ten feet in front of the Brijjen, a fair, and polite distance he approved of.

"I am Master Phann, leader of Sanctuary and the Underground Court. May I know who I am addressing?" again his low rumble could be heard across the awaiting army. The Haven voice had evolved for long distance communication and Phann used it well.

"I am Yasuko, this is my Haven Explorer ship. We received your distress call; we have come to help."

"We thank you, we are struggling to feed the Haven within our city. When your vessel was spotted, we hoped you may have a way to aide us. I fear there may be many deaths in the coming months. Each loss hurts us all." Phann clicked his claws and Zzind stepped forward. She was shaking like a leaf and the fury rose in Phann, hot and vile. The show of weakness was typical for a tree dweller.

I will have your skin upon my wall and drink your powdered scales, Zzind.

"We have a gift of welcome, Legion Arbiter Zzind if you please." Zzind unsteadily stepped forward, forcing herself to take each stride as she got closer to the plated guards. She brought up Phann's gift, a beautifully carved Rhumba, the traditional instrument of the Haven that complimented their low thrumming voices.

"Yasuko, we have no gift. If this is to go well, we must provide something as a show of respect," stated Finn over his radio. The army had taught him how to develop community relations and he was kicking himself for not thinking of it earlier.

"I'm not sure what we have."

Zuri cut in from the ship. "Is that cloak what I think it is, are all those data plaques stuck and sewn together?"

"Yes," answered Yasuko, "though they are all dead, just ghosts with no charge. I absorbed all of those recovered from the Orbital Station and the broken ship. I can make more but it will take too much time. We have Xxar's, but I promised him we would find a suitable place for it."

"Can we let them have a child? Even though it's a copy."

"It's not giving them a child, he lied knowing I wouldn't be able to tell you unless you asked, worried you wouldn't agree. It's an earlier copy of Xxar before he went mad. Before the genocide. He wants to come back without the guilt." Bitterness oozed from Yasuko's words. "But I have to leave it somewhere safe with the potential for him to study."

"Nothing safer than amongst his own people, and if we get the SeedShip, he can help teach them. Win, win."

"There is no wonder you humans get in so much trouble."

"It's a talent."

"I thank you for this beautiful gift, Master Phann. Your generosity is much appreciated and fitting with your standing. My honour guard is bringing out a suitable offering in return."

Phann watched the image, expecting it to squirm under its political misstep but it held its nerve. But why send the image of itself? Does it fear the surface as well, or is the air still so much of a concern it does not risk itself?

That seems the most likely, I just wish I knew its heritage. Most were tree dwellers, but some scientists had crossed castes if the Histories were true.

Another of the tall, armoured guards appeared from the door, striding over to the Haven projection. In its hand, on a shimmering piece of material, sat a square blue metalled plaque. Phann's heart leapt a little, the greed reaching his eyes before he pushed it away and reformed his expression. Zzind accepted the gift, clearly avoiding the touch of the guard and keeping the cloth between her and the plaque.

One for the collection, maybe.

"Master Phann, we may have the means to help you with your problem, and possibly much more. However, it will not be now, patience will be needed. We offer you all the technology we have at our disposal, but we must first find a vessel like mine for you. It will teach you all you need, and we will ensure it starts with food production. The sooner we leave for Mount Zezzat, the quicker we can return and help fully."

"We were hoping to host you as honoured guests, but yes, we would accept such a tremendous offer. If you can secure our future, then a little more time is a small price to pay." Master Phann turned his hands upside down on the reins of his Brijjen, the signal for stand down. This was shaping up nicely for his name to have its own chapter in the Histories. The offer was hugely generous, and one he mistrusted completely. They would drip feed him morsels in return for something, no one gave away such a position of power unless it gave you more in return. And no one but him got to control his people.

"We will return within a few days. If we are successful, then we will bring a SeedShip with us. If not we will go hunting elsewhere but be assured we will help."

Yasuko and the three guards turned and strode to their ship, Master Phann admired the arrogance that came with their obvious power and technology. But he would have it, and now he knew where they were going. Zezzat was an old name, shortened to Zzat over time but the Histories stated the building that still stood there was from before the Fall. So prominent was it, and linked with the Scientocracy, that the Masters stationed an Elite Legionnaire Pack there for millennia. And now Phann tested his newest weapons there, away from Sanctuary just in case anything went wrong, or the people found out how he spent much needed resources under the forbidden sky.

Yasuko's ship hovered, pulling in its legs to slot away in the undercarriage. Phann admired its lines once again, having hated the sky for so long it might just be time to change his ways.

Having stripped off their protective armour they all met back in the control room, Yasuko with them.

"That went well," said Noah, "the last-minute gift seemed to give him a lift."

"At least we made contact, and we now know they have built themselves up from the depths Xxar left them in. I think we may be able to do them some good," replied Finn, "if we can find a SeedShip like Yasuko says."

"It gives me some hope, and despite their proposed patience I am eager to find them an answer. I don't like their militaristic tendencies, but they have scraped themselves up from near extinction and must have lived in those tunnels ever since. I am unsure why they haven't emerged from the dark somewhat more."

Zuri stretched, her legs still bruised and sore from the Brijjen's pincers. "I'd suggest we get some food and rest. I ache all over and if we're to be ready for the mountains, we'll need to prep tomorrow. Yasuko, can we take it steady and scout the mountains tomorrow whilst we decide what we need? And see if you can turn up any information on the place, though I'm guessing there'll be no schematic if it's as important as you say."

CHAPTER 20

Sanctuary Underground City, Havenhome

"Master Phann, you wanted to see me?" Zzind was flanked by the honour guard who'd been sent to fetch her.

"Yes, Zzind I do. Walk with me," replied Phann, leading Zzind through his sanctum towards the rear. "I have something you need to see." He gestured for Zzind to go through the door to his private bedchamber.

The scales along her neck ruffle tingled, the false smile and posture of Master Phann shouting for her to run. But where? Zzind stepped through, Master Phann following behind shutting the door on the guards.

"We need to discuss a few things about the wonderful events today, your insights would be useful to compare against my thoughts. This way." He gestured towards another door set in the back, Zzind breathing a heavy sigh as they passed his nestbed. At least that was one issue she wouldn't have to deal with. Phann opened the door to a wide corridor beyond, one she did not recognise. The surface was bronzed metal, not the usual stone or hardened Tremal floor. It was beautiful, though Zzind wondered at its lack of lustre, as if uncared for. The walls were a blue hue, again metal and it reminded her of some of the older rooms they used for food storage deeper under the old city. As her hands touched the wall, she felt the same coldness that preserved the dried pupae so well. They soon reached a double door struck from the same metal with a panel by its side.

"No one alive has seen this room except myself, Zzind. I am taking you in to my confidence as I believe you are now ready to know what I know. Shall we?" Master Phann placed his palm upon the panel, it glowed a deeper blue and the door seal hissed. "After you."

Zzind pushed the left-hand door inwards, walking through to be greeted by a vast cavern. No tunnel or room in Sanctuary could match its size, and ordered in rows within were huge spaceships matching the size of the Explorer ship they had seen that day. Zzind expected many things beyond the door, including a skinning chair, but not this. Stunned, the needle pierced between her arm scales before she could react.

"Works every time, you tree dwellers are so stupid." Phann stepped back, letting the drug take its effect, losing count of how many times he'd done the same thing. Hundreds? He grabbed Zzind's arms and dragged her across to the nearest ship, shoving her against the hull wall. Still awake she could now see the fabled skinning chair, hidden behind the next ship, the blades, and shears hung along its edge. "Plenty of time for that Zzind. Your pathetic performance today was just too much, you are Haven, not a cowering cur."

Phann reached up to the hull wall she leant against, stroking the blue metal. Lust and greed flickered across his face, not the mask he'd shown the Scientist but his true self. He slipped off the ceremonial cloak he still wore, placing it next to Zzind.

"These are people, Zzind. Copies of dead Haven from before the Fall. Hard to believe isn't it, but the Masters have been wearing ghosts. Each time one is found they would bring it here and place it on the ship hull, hoping it would open the riches within. And when it didn't, add it to the cloak. A sign of status but also failure, a heavy burden I carry. None have been found in my time as Master, I thought I'd never get the chance. But here I am with you, an opportunity to celebrate with my favourite pastime."

Phann placed the square plaque against the ship hull, expectant of failure but pleased to at least have taken his place properly amongst the Masters. The hull responded with a blue glow, a low hum emanating from the metal. A sequence of lights played further along its surface.

"What? I've done it, I have opened the box of treats. Do you see Zzind, it's alive."

Zzind celebrated by slipping the blade between Phann's back scales, digging deep and twisting the hooked blade into his organs before ripping across his spine.

"Do you see, Master Phann? Did you look carefully enough with those sadist's eyes at what was before you? They were humans, Phann. Humans who brought the Fall down upon us. It is their filth that destroyed us, that allowed the Masters to rise and degrade and kill at will. They reduced us to living like worms in the dark. Humans, and the pretty trinket they gave you and the promises of food blinded you to the truth. They are back, and they are here to finish what they started. Extinction, and I will not allow it."

Zzind withdrew the knife and plunged it into Phann's neck, panting with rage and ire. The ship door opened as she slid the knife out, wiping it on the ceremonial cloak. The antidote surging through her system well worth the bribes she had paid. Zzind looked towards the beckoning door. It offered salvation in the face of the human threat, a salvation Phann did not deserve and would never see.

CHAPTER 21

Mountains of Zezzat, Havenhome

"They selected the position because of very low geological movement, with the mountain growth steady but low, and built it from an alloy bonded rock that would shape and move with any tectonic activity. The high Zezzat Valley has a history of powerful winds but there is little dust for it to erode the rock or the building. Most erosion is by freeze and thaw activity," detailed Yasuko.

"So what do we have down there?" asked Zuri, pointing to the lower section of the screen around the flat roofed Data Storage building.

"That's a huge rockfall, probably with all the erosion of the mountain and shifting of the rivers it's undercut the rock-face. From the initial ground penetrating scans the roof is stable but it won't take the ship's weight, after thirty-three thousand years it's surprising that it's not all buried," stated Noah.

"No, that there. Can we switch to thermal?" Yasuko obliged. "That is a gun emplacement, multiple thermal signatures all positioned to support, our flyover spooked them. Seen it enough times, if we focus the camera down further on visual, I'm betting we have a piece of artillery with soldiers in position to reload. If there's one, there will be more."

"I've taken the basic thermal layout and overlaid similar signatures on to the main overhead view." Yasuko pulled the picture back to show the entire valley. "Four gun emplacements sat round the building."

"There's a little overhead camouflage but they've clearly no clue," chipped in Finn. "We've seen nothing mechanical that flies, just a few large-winged animals, I'm betting they knew we were coming, and it's a rush job."

"On my assessment, I think we need to park and walk in. We can't use the space near the building as we'll be sitting ducks. I'm guessing that even this ship under sustained artillery fire won't last long, Yasuko?" Yasuko nodded, Smith continued, "So we need to walk in and use all the advantages we have. Thermal, night vision and long-range weaponry. But if they are dug in, there's bound to be more."

"Yasuko, there's every chance these Haven are hostile. We saw the greeting party, and the hidden ambush; they are desperate and desperate people make stupid decisions. If they attack, we will be forced to kill, so it's decision time. The more prepared we are, the better weaponry we have, the less of the Haven we will have to kill. It won't stop us handing over a SeedShip, your people need help, but we want to get through this alive."

Yasuko shifted uncomfortably, another human gesture. All eyes rested upon her, waiting on an answer.

"You want me to supply equipment that will hurt my people? My programming forbids this, I am shackled. And even if I wasn't what you are asking goes against everything I regard as right. I cannot."

"I will defend me and mine above all else, Yasuko, but will you?" Zuri, leaning on the central console, stood up and walked out. Finn followed, sparing Yasuko a thoughtful glance as he did so. Noah remained, studying Yasuko carefully as Smith turned himself off in a fury.

"Noah, I... What did she mean? I don't understand."

"She means you are part of her crew, that she would defend you as much as she would Finn or I, even Smith. Have you noticed she always asks you? She never orders you. Once you are under Zuri's wing you are protected for life. And if it means anything to you, we all feel the same. We're risking our lives to find a way home, and to help your people."

"I am an AI, Noah, I am not alive. Why would you care about me?"

"I can't answer that, it's something you will have to discover for yourself. I strongly believe you will eventually understand now that you have finally asked the question yourself." Noah paused whilst Yasuko took in what he said. "And as for helping us, I have some ideas that may not break the Convention or your shackles."

CHAPTER 22

Spaceship, Sanctuary Underground City, Havenhome

Zzind sat with her back to the cold, blue-tinged wall of the console, her mind reeling. For most of the night and morning she conversed with the ship's voice, and she was at a loss at what to do next. The ship called itself an AI, and only remembered up to the time of landing at the original city, some thirty-three thousand years ago. It had been recalled by the Haven Convention to bring the Scientist Caste back for a debate demanded by the Restoration Faction. After the crew did not return, and when all outside communication stopped, the ship shut itself down only to be awoken by Master Phann and his data plaque.

But it hadn't ended there, Zzind explained the events after the recall as were written in the Histories. The arrival of the scientists and their subsequent killing by the Restoration, and the humans that sent down a squalid spaceship filthy with microorganisms leading to the Fall. Then how the Haven were saved by the Masters and the Undercourt, who rallied the survivors and brought them to Sanctuary and the under city, where train and worm tunnels became their homes.

The AI requested to ask questions, and Zzind did her best to answer. But then it shook her to her core, testing the air outside the AI told her it was just as infected as it probably was after the Fall. The air was rife with life that multiplied and took over their planet, and she was just as likely to be so too. Zzind denied this, and asked to be tested but the only way that could be done, with the crew dead, was to agree to become Ship's crew and undergo the full analysis.

Zzind looked at her hand, the skin pink, and the gel solidifying within the hole in her wrist. Even now the tears welled, the thought of human filth within her causing despair and anguish.

What am I? A vessel for human disease, dirty on the inside as well as the out.

"Ship, the metal plaque Phann used to get in, is it like a key? If I leave, will it let me back in?"

"It woke me up, but it is not a key. It contains a copy of Science Officer Xxar, the Haven who oversaw the Orbital Station."

"A copy? You mean a picture?"

"No, his complete DNA sequence, body information, and memories up to the point he was copied. We use them for rebirth, bringing them back to life in a new body," the mechanical voice replied.

"Can I speak to him? Will he report where I am to the Undercourt?"

"Science Officer Xxar will not know who the Undercourt is, but yes, he would likely have to do that, and my communication system can connect with the radios in Sanctuary. If you put the plaque in the dais recess you are leaning on his copy will appear."

"Why haven't you called the Undercourt in?"

"You were under attack and initially I thought you acted in self-defence. Your body scan showed you already had the antidote in your body, but your description of the man and my scanning of the radio signals has confirmed what he was like, I stand by my decision based on the safety of you as Haven and crew. And as crew, you tell me what to do."

"Could you block Xxar calling out then, if I told you to?"

"At first, but he has an override capability, I was there when he used it on an AI back before the Orbital Station was built."

Anguish overwhelming her, Zzind put her head in her hands and sobbed. Stuck in a spaceship that could not help, with her only chance a ghost imprinted on a metal plaque. Here she was bursting to tell all of Haven they were free to go the surface, free to feel the sun on their faces, yet disgusted with the filth in her own body. And who would believe a murderer, anyway?

"Zzind, your body signs show high anguish and stress. You have not eaten since yesterday, nor slept. I can provide food and a bed."

Sobbing, Zzind replied through wet fingers, "Thank you, Ship. That would be good."

CHAPTER 23
Mountains of Zezzat, Havenhome

"Zuri, may we speak?" asked Yasuko as Zuri slipped on her backpack over her cold weather coat.

"Yes, Yasuko. We can talk."

"I spoke to Noah after you left yesterday. He explained what you meant about 'me and mine'. I have not got my thoughts straight; it has confused me greatly. But part of me thinks I should thank you, so here I am. Thank you."

Zuri looked Yasuko up and down, pleased to get through to Yasuko though it was only the beginning of a long process. However, it would not help them with what was coming.

"That's okay, Yasuko. We are all changing through this, and none of us are finding it easy."

Kupotea njia ndiyo kujua njia. And to get lost is to learn the way.

"Noah also pushed me to help, I think he was trying to get around the Convention rules but I couldn't agree to everything he suggested because they would harm the Haven soldiers directly. However, these may help." A section of the wall next to Zuri folded in on itself, revealing five metal discs "There is one for each of you, they will provide additional power for your armour. In future I may do this for your weapons, but not today. The other two are for Smith to ensure enough energy for the tasks ahead."

Zuri smiled. "It's a start, Yasuko, but it won't stop me asking." She took the plaques, and asked, "So longer, faster, higher?"

"Yes, by about forty per cent. But your body and the suits

won't be able to take the stress of much more than that, anyway."

"Okay Noah, Finn, Yasuko has a new toy for you." Zuri handed out the discs as Yasuko showed them where to place it on the inside of their left arm. "We haven't trained with these so be careful, it will increase your running speed, jumping and landing ability by forty per cent for a short time but your body will be affected. Use them only if you must."

"Right," said Finn, "I'm on point, Zuri at the rear. It's cold and we will reach the snow line in about a mile. After that it'll be hard going, we'll judge on crampons and rope then. We're carrying heavy packs with the weather change so the pace will be steady, let's get going."

Finn led them through the airlock to be greeted by wind and falling snow. Luckily, it was blowing from behind at the moment but in the mountains things could change quickly. His army cold mountain training was as limited as Zuri's, just the basics, but he knew his way round an ice axe from his days of Munro bagging in Scotland. Besides, it was better than sweating in the jungle, especially as there were absolutely no Brijjen in the mountains. Just a few local predators of an easier size to deal with, but no less ferocious according to Yasuko (he remembered to ask this time). Smith was primed, aware that one of them, the Cryzen a four-foot bear like creature with two rows of serrated teeth, had such a low body temperature it might not register.

Finn tried to pick out the route as they came to the first rockfalls, Smith guiding him along what he judged to be the easiest path. Clambering over he could see the rise in front of him, leading to the mouth of the valley between the two peaks of Mt Zezzat and Mt Teq. Thirty-three thousand years ago they would have been walking along a road, now time had eroded all of that away but still there was a defined route, and the most obvious for an ambush.

Finn reckoned they'd be looking at sixty minutes up to the snow line that started just below the valley mouth. Beyond that probably sixty more depending on snow levels. At least it wasn't glaciated, now that would have been tricky. What bothered him was the lack of support weapons, limiting their options with no back up sidearms should the *weapons of choice* run out. He had mused over Noah's decision to go for the AW50F sniper rifle that had saved their skins back on Earth, but in the end he agreed it was a good option. It just left Noah in difficulty with close quarter combat, so Finn made sure he was ladened with some extra flashbangs as a backup.

When we're off Havenhome I'm going to have a serious word with Yasuko about storing up some heavy-hitting equipment.

"How we doing, Smith?"

"Oh now you want to talk to me, thought you were ignoring me all this time."

"Well, the peace was good while it lasted but you might actually be useful right now."

"You know when I die properly, you are on my 'most haunted' list. Every night, whispering in your ear."

"Make a change from all day. Anything to report, Corporal."

"Nope, all clear as far as I can tell on thermal and visual, about a hundred yards range up slope. I've been experimenting with radar but not so good in this type of terrain. Might supplement the air movement sensor in the future though. You thinking an ambush just as we hit the snowline, where we might be slowed down or be changing footwear?"

"Yep, not thought about the crampon change but likely. They'll have a view downslope, but it'll come down to what range they have. In this gravity it should be less for comparable rounds. Going to be difficult to judge with not knowing their level of tech."

"Woah, contact. Slow moving up above at that hundred yard line. Very low thermal image but warmer than the rocks. That Cryzen thing I reckon, and there's another, and another. Think we got mum

and cubs on the move."

Finn signalled stop, they had agreed to stay off the radio until they understood the Haven tech level or if things were getting hairy, whichever came first. Binoculars out, and thanking Yasuko for them, he tracked to where Smith guided him to look via his visor. There was the faint but obvious image of the Cryzen mother, and about twice the size Yasuko had described.

Evolution for you, and no Haven to share the food.

He watched as it ambled across their path, angling up towards the edge of the valley mouth nearest Mount Zezzat. Give it ten minutes and they'll be out of our way, no need for us to be concerned. Finn called up Noah, leaving Zuri at the rear, setting him up to scan the valley mouth with that rifle of his. Might as well do something useful while they waited.

CHAPTER 24

Spaceship, Sanctuary Underground City, Havenhome

"Zzind, there is something you need to hear," said the Ship.

Fed and rested Zzind already sat in the console room having come to her decision. Between all her choices the only one she could see was to persuade the Undercourt about the human delivered organisms that lived in all the air, including Sanctuary. Bring them to the ship, let them talk to it and hear the truth for themselves.

"Okay Ship, what is it?"

"The Undercourt elected a new Master, Master Yasque. He announced over the radio news that you must have escaped above ground or thrown yourself in to one of the vent fans because you cannot be found."

"It's a trick, one I used in the past. They want to flush me out." Zzind ruffled her neck scales.

Time to be brave.

"Can you connect with their radio? Let them know I am here, and I have news for them."

"All the radios or just Master Yasque's private frequency?"

Zzind toyed with the idea to announce her find all over Sanctuary now she knew it was possible, but they'd just declare her mad and point to Phann's murder as evidence.

"Private line, to come here to this room and this spaceship. Alone. He has ten minutes."

"As you wish," the disembodied voice replied. "Done."

Zzind paced the room for nine of those ten minutes desperately racking her mind for a way out of this. They needed to hear the Ship, and to do that she would need Yasque to come inside. But that was the danger, would he? And if so, she doubted he would be alone.

Why did I rush this?

"Master Yasque is outside."

"Alone? Armed?"

"No, he has four guards outside the entrance door. They are armed. There is one woman alongside him, though she does not appear armed I cannot guarantee that, nor can I with Master Yasque. They may have hidden inert weapons."

"When I say can you open the door, keeping the airlock door closed. Invite them both inside, say who you are. Tell them you saw what happened, and that I was defending myself. That you have spoken to me about many things, and they need to listen to what I have to say. Okay, do it."

And I hope I missed nothing.

"They are arguing about coming in, though they both appear desperate to do so. They want the guards to wait at the hull door."

"Agreed."

After a few seconds Ship spoke again, "They are inside, and I am telling them what you asked. They are hyper anxious because of my activation and the 'murder' of Master Phann."

"Next tell them to throw any weapons out the door, that you will know if they are lying. Then that you will open the airlock door, but the outside door will shut for my safety. They may then come in; you will ensure their safety."

"They have both thrown a handgun out the door, and a small knife from the Master. I think greed overcame their fears. Shall

I open the airlock?" With Zzind's agreement the seal broke and the door opened. Zzind recognised the woman instantly, she was of tree dweller stock but a spy in the political games the Undercourt played. They assumed she wouldn't know, but Zzind had played their games for years. She took her place on the other side of the console, keeping a distance from the pair.

"Legion Arbiter Zzind," said Yasque, "this voice we hear claims you are innocent of murder, that Phann was attempting to kill you. Come with us, we can straighten this out with the Undercourt. The truth always wins out."

"No, I don't think I'd last a second out there. I know the game, Master Yasque, and I won't be allowed to live. Whether by trial or accident, I'll be dead before I can speak. Especially as the Undercourt turned a blind eye to his hobby." Zzind watched Yasque's reaction, knowing full well she was right. "I've brought you here so you can listen to the Ship. It has examined the air, and me, we are all immersed in the human filth. However hard that may be to bear we can at least leave Sanctuary and live in the sun again."

"Utter nonsense, drivel. Take the word of what? A voice from the past. This ship is an asset, a prize and we'll thrive with the technology it provides. And someday, we can clean the air above and then we will be free. But not until the Undercourt decrees it, not this thing." Yasque gesticulated at the surrounding Ship, his eyes full of the same greed and his heart the same political need to control as Master Phann.

"Then you have wasted your time here, leave. I will tell Sanctuary myself. Ship can you broadca…" Zzind didn't get the chance to complete her words as the spy's knife flew towards her, the blade glinting in the ceiling's glow. Zzind watched in horror as death approached, defenceless and untrained it would pierce her throat and take her last breath.

But then it stopped, inches from her neck it hovered in space, with her last breath held against the expected pain and death.

"You have attacked a member of my crew, and another Haven with intent to harm," Ship's welcome voice reverberated around the room. "You are to leave immediately." The floor rose in front of Zzind's eyes, a ripple of bronzed metal four feet high that pushed against Yasque and the spy, shoving them through the airlock and beyond as the outside door opened then slammed shut.

"Ship, I don't know what I just saw but thank you."

"It is my duty and prerogative to protect crew and Haven. I could not let them come to harm either. This was the safest way, though unfortunate. Science Officer Xxar's plaque was taken before she threw the knife."

"Lock them out?"

"I cannot, as I said before."

"I need to leave," shouted Zzind in panic.

"Leaving, engines starting, and we are rising. Yasque and companion are running for the corridor. May I ask where we are leaving to?"

CHAPTER 25

Mountains of Zezzat, Havenhome

"Got them?"

"Yep, two on the left side about seventy yards from the valley mouth. Two more to the right at about eighty-five yards from it. I can hit them from here if the rifle compensates for the gravity. But I won't know until I try. They have crude looking rifles with very long barrels. Beat this baby by a good eighteen inches, held up on V-shaped rods."

"Smith how far are they?"

"About six hundred yards, weapons like those could shoot that distance accurately on Earth around the time of the First World War. I'm betting we are just about on the edge of their range with the extra-long barrel increasing muzzle velocity. But I'm guessing."

"Maybe we lucked out with momma Cryzen then. They haven't shot us yet. Zuri? What are you thinking?"

"I'm thinking we need to know if they are hostile, if they are then Noah takes them out. I am not risking our arses. Soldiers are soldiers and death comes with service. They shoot, we shoot back harder. Remember we are the aliens here, and we've come armed. I doubt they'll make the same mistake as Lieutenant Bhakshi."

"If we go up cautious, dodging from cover to cover they'll assume we are the hostile ones anyway, we would. We have no choice, minimise ourselves as targets but keep the weapons down. We don't shoot until we have a clear picture, radios on as they'll see us soon enough." Zuri and Noah nodded agreement,

Finn set the new pace, moving amongst the boulder debris strewn across the route. He glanced back to make sure Noah was keeping his head down, this was open country in an area of combat he'd never trained in. Keeping to the right of Zuri he advanced to different cover each time, Zuri in his ear again keeping him calm and talking it through.

They made another two hundred yards when the first shot rang out. The sound echoed around the peaks, much louder than their old SA80s back on Earth. The round zipped into the ground between Finn and Zuri, about ten feet from each.

"Warning shot, or simply a poor one. Keep going, let's see what happens," said Finn.

A second shot then a third rang out, bouncing off boulders nearest Finn, spraying chips of stone on to his visor as he ducked down.

"Guess that answers the question. Zuri can you find a safe place for Noah to shoot from."

"On it." Zuri scanned the rockfalls until she spotted an area with three tumbled boulders leaning against each other, gaps between. An infantry sniper with a modern weapon could make a pinpoint strike through those gaps but it would be safer than shooting over a rock. Zuri radioed Noah, pointing out the formation. As Noah moved, she sprinted hoping to confuse those watching and a target running sideways at speed was harder to hit. Zuri slid along the boulder she'd chosen for cover as another round rang out, she never heard where it hit.

Unwieldy weapons, but I bet if they hit you stay hit.

"Okay Noah, these Haven are soldiers. They are attempting to kill us. You are potentially saving our lives by doing this, and if they have any sense, they'll stop and move on when that cannon fires." Zuri waited, no response but she could hear Noah calming his breathing, "You good?"

"Yeah, I'm good. Just thought our First Contact would be

different, but it all just seems to come down to fighting. Doesn't matter what planet you are on; someone is always too frightened or too greedy to hold out the hand of friendship. But you're right, they chose to be here and are attempting to kill us. We deal with that first."

Zuri waited for the first high calibre round to fly, she needed to be ready for Noah. On Earth he'd been there for them against aliens who had attacked first and killed their fellow soldiers, saving their lives. Much harder to take a life when you could choose to walk away. Before long the echo of the shot bounced round the boulders, much quieter than the Haven's it faded quickly. It was swiftly followed by a second, then a little later a third.

"The fourth soldier is on the run, I took out the two to the right though one may only be injured as it was a shoulder hit. The other was to the left, definite kill but his companion upped and ran for it." Zuri noted he didn't say whether he could have taken him out as he ran away.

"Let's move at speed, Smith keep a close eye." Finn waited for Noah to signal ready and set off across the boulder field, eager to reach the valley mouth before any reinforcements could pin them down again. Ignoring the cover, he sped up the incline towards the right-hand gun emplacement desperate to ensure that soldier was out of action. Zuri and Noah continued to follow procedure, using the boulders as cover and falling behind.

"Remember your discipline, Finn. I can feel that adrenaline pumping, and this would have been a killing field with modern rifles, but charging in will not keep your squad alive. By the—"

"Numbers," finished Finn, slowing down and changing his tactics as he sought cover. "Hate saying you're right, Smith."

"Oh, I think you can say it, I'm waiting..."

His back to a rough-edged boulder, Finn took a breather as he held back for Noah and Zuri. It only took ten seconds, but time enough for huge consequences in combat. As he watched, Zuri and Noah hit the floor almost simultaneously.

"Got a thermal now it's moved from behind that stonework. One alive but there's blood signature pouring everywhere."

Finn turned, holding his rifle out he tried to get a picture using the mirror sight that had been so useful looking round corners in the Orbital Station. Not the best tool at a distance but he made out a figure leaning on the rocks, sword in hand.

What a crazy world this is.

"Zuri, cover." Finn moved out from the boulder, rifle to his eye as he walked towards the Haven soldier, remaining quiet as his babbling speech would only cause more panic. Its breathing was extremely shallow, the altitude not helping the lungs in the desperate battle for air. Blood poured from a shattered left shoulder, the arm loose at its side. It wore no armour, just heavy clothes against the cold with its scaled neck and face exposed. The sword shook as pain and the blue blood loss hit home. Finn waved the gun to show he should put the sword down, then used his left-hand palm out when it didn't respond. The light left its eyes as the soldier died in front of him. Finn felt relief, not wanting to kill a wounded fellow soldier and knowing full well that restraining it would have been a worse way to die in this cold and with the blood loss.

"Clear," he called on the radio.

Finn scanned the sniper nest, they had camouflaged it with a wooden frame with rocks above and around. A firepit sat in one corner, the fire out and the room bitter cold. Glancing over the weapons they looked very much like older versions of hunting rifles, the wood working, and milling of the barrel looked high quality work. Single bolt action that seemed ungainly, but then again their hands were different and likely it was hooked for their longer digit. The round was huge, worrying Finn about the effect on their ceramic plating. Finn showed the shell to Zuri, who frowned with concern. On the floor next to the ammunition a telescope lay splattered with blue blood.

Noah was knelt over the other Haven soldier, shaking a little. Zuri touched Finn's elbow, signalling towards Noah.

My turn.

He walked over, and crouched next to Noah, placing his hand on his shoulder. The past few weeks were hitting home, the battles they'd faced just to survive. Noah was an academic, out to do his bit as part of the army reserves and thrust in to taking life. Zuri recognised the moment, one Finn had been through and fallen deep into the pit of PTSD. Right now, he was in a better place, though it hovered at the fringes of his mind every second of every day. Zuri was his counterbalance, but when she was threatened his mind still overwhelmed him. But everyone was different, and Noah teetered on his own edge at this moment.

"You're going to tell me it's necessary. We have no choice if we are to get home or help the rest of their people despite killing their soldiers. It hurts, Finn, however it's presented."

"Yeah, it does. And you know the answers, can analyse them all to the end of the world. But we are human, Noah, and that means we can choose to do the right thing even when it damages us. Morality is not black and white; it is streaked with grey. None of us comes away clean. But as long as you have a firm belief in why you are doing it then at least you have a chance to get through it." Finn squeezed Noah's shoulder as he got up.

I think he's tougher than he believes, but it doesn't make this any easier.

CHAPTER 26

Spaceship, Sanctuary Underground City, Havenhome

Shuddering, the ship lifted above the others in the hangar. Bringing the engines up to hover, it scanned the hanger doors with trepidation. Beyond them it expected thirty-three thousand years of change. The AI named as Ship by Zzind, eased the engines forward mindful of the guards scattering below. It ran through the nanobot levels, most had survived the dormancy, but they were about eighty per cent capacity. Hopefully enough if things went wrong.

"Just get us out of here, we can decide when we are free," said Zzind as she instinctively curled herself in a ball on the floor, wrapped in protective scales as her fear hit. They were flying.

"On it," replied Ship as it activated the doors, surprised to see them respond immediately. As they split, mud and building debris fell through, scattering along the bronzed floor. Ground penetrating radar showed they were sixty feet down, better than Ship judged though from what Zzind had told her the Haven had used much of the old city as building blocks for the tunnels underneath. Bringing the bow debris cannons online Ship began to methodically blast a path through and upwards. It wasn't pretty, they'd never been designed for this type of work but needs must. Ship had been told to leave and leave it would.

Five minutes of blasting enabled enough room ahead that it was safe to use the smaller of the asteroid deflection missiles. Again checking that the hanger was clear first, the projectile streaked onward and upward fracturing the last of the debris and light cracked through the gap above the slagged stone tunnel.

"Leaving, please strap into the chair." Zzind took her place in the chair that appeared from the floor, the straps materialising from nowhere wrapping round her and locking her in. She felt panic rise within but held it back. The Ship had done nothing but protect her and intended to take her to the sky she longed for.

Ship narrowed, bringing in the outer hull and elongating slightly with nanobots at the bow reinforcing the hull. Pushing the engines onward, they eased through the doors and up through the earth eventually emerging in the light above. Ship gave an inward sigh, the nanobots were down to forty per cent. Enough to be within safety boundaries, but it soon needed to manufacture more.

Scanning the area as it broke into the sky, Ship noted how little there was left of the city it had known so well. The layout could be discerned, but no buildings remained. Its sensors found the mineral deposits required and taking 'leave' as a destination plotted the thousand-mile course to the only place on Havenhome where palladium reached the surface.

"We have left Sanctuary and are on a heading eastwards. With your permission I need to rebuild my nanobots otherwise we will be outside safety parameters."

"Permission granted," said Zzind, not understanding a word of what Ship meant. "Am I able to see us fly?" A screen appeared in the wall showing three different views of their flightpath. It took a while, but Zzind overcame the vertigo it induced and began to almost enjoy the view. "How long will it take?"

"A few hours flight. I need to be careful with my fuel levels, and then probably another half a day to recover the palladium. I can fly and manufacture at the same time, however, we will need a destination."

The Mountains of Zezzat? Then back to Sanctuary with the Ship to free her people? Zzind felt overwhelmed by it all, her thoughts constantly returning to the filth in her veins.

CHAPTER 27

Mountains of Zezzat, Havenhome

Conditions got a little tougher at the snowline. The wind immediately picked up, and increased further as they reached the lip of the rise, welcoming them to the valley mouth. It was spectacular, the valley edges rose sharply, and the peaks glinted as the sun hit their icy edges. But the snow whipped up around them, intermittently blinding their view as gusts reached fifty miles an hour before dropping in an instant to nothing. At least there was no ice formation to battle through, they kept their crampons off and resisted the temptation to tie together for now though any stronger wind might change Finn's mind as he leaned into another gust.

"What we got Smith? Any signs on those sensors of yours now we are on the flat?"

"Yep, they are using rocks as cover ahead but thermal shows them when they shift position, and there are some stone-built buildings across our route I can pick up if I zoom in. Fortifications and barracks from the design, attached to the front of the Data Storage building. I can pick up two of the artillery placements."

"They will have been setting markers for those, using the valley floor as a range finder. Look out for any impact craters everyone. When they start we are in range and that ups the ante. They may well choose to go for drawing us in and hitting us with sniper and artillery fire." Finn carried on, eyeing the terrain for any tell-tales of heavy ordnance.

We are going to have to use our advantage to drive them to ground. No option but to overwhelm them, make them fear us from a distance or they'll pound us to dust. Maybe Noah's right to worry about what we are doing.

Pushing on through the wind and driven snow for another hundred yards Finn fretted about the snow cover, at this rate impact craters may well be covered or at least partially hidden. Amongst the swirls he could make out the odd footprint of the retreating Haven soldier. At least he hadn't gone high, that would have caused another headache he could do without.

"Finn," called Zuri, "just ahead of you, to the right. That boulder is cracked open, and it doesn't look old. Are those burn marks along its surface?"

A whistling sound broke through as the wind suddenly dropped again.

"Incoming!" shouted Smith over the radio. "Down and cover."

Shrapnel flew alongside shattered stone as they hit the ground, piercing Zuri and Finn's thick coats but stopped by their armour. Unscathed, Noah was further back and now behind cover.

"Smith can you pick these up?"

"No, bit of a heat signature but by the time it's in my range it'll be too late."

A second whistle split the air, and Finn moved sideways in the hope it would hit the same spot. An explosion threw him forward and smack into the boulder he was aiming for. The impact dazed him briefly, the shrapnel shredding the back of his coat.

"Finn?" shouted Zuri.

"I'm alive, head hurts. We need to move."

A rifle shot cut through the wind, nearby and familiar, followed quickly by a second and a third. There was a respite before another two shots rang out.

"Noah?" enquired Finn.

"Busy." A sixth shot rang out. "I've hit a few but the distance and wind are an issue. The others have gone to ground. I think the placement on the right flank is out of action, but there's at least two soldiers still operational on the left."

"We move, all of us, on a diagonal to the right. Go." Finn watched for their movement, when happy they were in motion, he followed with Zuri in the lead. Moving as quickly as the snow and rock litter would allow, the motorised armour supported their ankles as they bent and twisted over uneven ground. Zuri reached a larger boulder field, rocks too big to climb over but they could slip in between for cover. She slipped into a space big enough for all of them and was swiftly joined by Noah then Finn, panting as they fought for breath in the freezing air.

"We move along this side, there should only be one big gun that will have our range soon from the back corner. Smith have you got the sniper placement locked in?"

"Yep, four hundred yards ahead. Judging by earlier combat I'd say that's about their rifle range in this gravity."

"Okay, Noah what's the power level on that rifle?" Noah showed him the stock, it was at thirty percent. "Enough to take out one gun emplacement. Your priority is the artillery piece at the back corner of the building where the large rockfall ends. Zuri, you take the sniper nest, best judgement on which rounds. I'll cover you both and Smith and I will watch the sky."

"Incoming," shouted Smith. The artillery shell smashing a boulder ten yards to their right shifting the whole cluster around them. "Can't stay here, that was the rearward unit finding its range. Another, but it's going to fall way short. That was the left side front unit." The shell exploded as Smith reported, "But they're good, we need to move."

"Up high on the valley side, as soon as you have a chance take the shot. No time." Finn allowed Zuri and Noah past, they scrambled along the edge of the boulder field and up the incline of the valley sides. Finn felt the itch at the back of his neck, this wasn't going well.

A whistle split the air, another just behind as Smith tried to warn them. The double hit smashing to the ground throwing Noah and Zuri sideways on to the top of rocks they had just left. Shrapnel and stone chips shredding the last of Finn's coat as he rocked backwards. The groans over the radio were a good sign as he clambered over the rocks towards his beleaguered fireteam.

"Zuri? Noah?" Finn's panic strewn voice echoed over the radio. Reaching Zuri first he could see no blood or twisted bones. Zuri moved as he placed a hand on her leg, turning and giving him a pained thumbs up. Noah stirred, rolling on to his back Finn could see the ruptured coat along his right side and shattered ceramic plates.

Close.

"Move, now Private. Move!" Finn dragged him backwards, engaging the additional power pack in his armour he pulled him up and over his shoulder racing for the valley side. Zuri followed, Noah's AW50 in her hand. Finn surged upwards aiming for a small cave inlet at the valley side, about twenty yards ahead, trusting Zuri to follow. Reaching the cave mouth he dropped Noah gently to the floor, checking for blood as he did so.

"I'm bruised, but okay. Where's my gun?" said Noah, clearly hurting but not incapacitated.

Zuri reached them both, handing the weapon over she turned and dropped to a crouched position, instantly sighting for the sniper emplacement. They were in the open and it wouldn't take them long. Noah eased himself next to her, ignoring the pain he calmed his breath. Zuri fired a three-round energy bolt burst that seared through the snow, followed by a single armour-piercing round that drilled through a wooden strut, bringing the roof down on any survivors. Zuri did not waiver, if anyone moved, she was ready.

Noah peered through his sight, it zoomed in through the

snowfall picking up the distant thermal signatures of the artillery crew and the glowing barrel of the big gun. It was about a thousand yards, but Noah poured the armour-piercing rounds into the emplacement, moving on to the next panicked soldier after each had fallen. As the last round sped to its target, the power meter ran dry.

"Incoming," shouted Smith, *"but short. We are out of their range on the left. Need to assess your fireteam, Corporal Finn."*

Finn didn't need reminding, but that was Smith for you.

"Report Zuri," he said.

"Bruised and battered right side. No broken bones, just a few fractured plates and my coat is screwed." Zuri picked out some ball bearings from the mess of her coat. "Nasty, these guys are not messing around. Rifle lost five percent power, armour at full."

"I'm as battered as Zuri with my plates shredded on the right-hand side, but nothing got through. Armour on full power. Weapon dead, just my knife, four flashbangs and a pack full of chemical explosives like you."

"Right, armour down to standard power so good for another three hours in this gravity. You're heavier than you look Noah. Rest is all fine. We need to get going, that barrage was heavy going but the firepower you gave back will spook them. Time to press that home."

CHAPTER 28

Sanctuary Underground City, Havenhome

Master Yasque followed behind his honour guard who had already scouted the large room containing the spaceships, his mind reeling after the events of the last few days. To have been thrust into power after positioning himself politically for so many years was just the start of the wonders he had experienced. The fall of Master Phann was much needed, his tastes disturbing the status quo of the Undercourt's power base, but now Yasque held the shiny blue plaque that had gained that last Master entry to one of the dormant spaceships. Never mind the loss of Zzind and that ship, there were nine more and the technology within could seal his power for a very long time. Yasque shifted the weight of the ceremonial cloak he hadn't stopped wearing since his inauguration.

If it doesn't work though, I will have to remember to have the guards killed before the truth gets out about the cache.

Master Yasque's chief confederate, the spy Bhkrin stalked beside him. She who had stolen the plaque from Zzind's ship and so nearly took her down. Together they had planned his rise to power, and in her case the driver being the status and money that came with it. But this was the first she knew of the spaceship cache and simply took it in her stride.

A strong female that one.

Yasque stopped at the next spaceship in the row, ignoring the open doors and smouldering tunnel beyond he placed the blue plaque upon the hull. To his delight the light sequence activated, and the door opened. The rush of adrenaline nearly made him misstep, but he calmed his excitement and walked on in.

"Hello," said a familiar sounding disembodied voice, "may I ask where my crew are?"

"That is a long story, one that may take some time in the telling." Yasque and Bhkrin stepped through as the airlock door opened. "But we have the time." The room they walked in reminded Yasque of Zzind's ship. The couches in the same place, the dais in the centre with its raised slab and recesses. Rooms went off in all directions and the smell of cleanliness surprised him after thirty-three thousand years.

"Do you have a name? I am Master Yasque, and this is Bhkrin, my advisor." Silence followed his question, and a sudden coldness swept the room as the warmth of the ceiling light faded in and out. The unease spread to Bhkrin, who shifted from foot to foot as her spine tingled with an edge of fear for the first time.

The voice cut back in, a stiff edge to it, "May I ask a question first, Master Yasque?"

"Of course," replied Yasque, weary with the mood shift but ever the political animal he could adapt and play for time.

"Why are you wearing some of my crew's replicas? I can sense their ghosts upon the damaged data plaques amongst so many others. Old ones, copies from before our last exploration, but still my crew."

"I...," replied Yasque in a panic, this was going spectacularly wrong. He needed to placate the voice, "I inherited these from the last Master, not knowing what they are. We have another, is this one of your crew?" Yasque proffered the plaque in his hand, not knowing where to look as the voice came from everywhere and nowhere.

"Analysing...that is Science Officer Xxar, and not a ghost copy but powered."

"Would you like it? If it helps?"

"My duty is to all Haven; I should rebirth him as is my obligation. If you place the plaque in the slot on the dais, I can begin the process."

Yasque breathed a sigh of relief, slotting Xxar's blue square of metal in the dais.

I will have this ship and its technology in no time.

CHAPTER 29

Mountains of Zezzat, Havenhome

Zuri sat with her torso squeezed between two low snow-covered rocks, thankful for her armour keeping her dry but beginning to feel the cold as her shredded jacket was next to useless. She had reached the snipers nest on the right-hand side, with a view of the opposite encamped pair who were playing hide and seek with Noah and Finn about two hundred yards behind her. Smith got a handle on their thermal movements, warning each of the pair when and how they were going to fire.

Another few minutes of that and they'll think we're ghosts.

Zuri brought up her sight, switching to thermal as her best option.

Sorry, but it's me and mine, or you. I choose us.

Zuri repeated the three-round burst into each of the snipers, then the armour-piercing round to the top to seal them in. She took no pleasure in it, it was necessary. That left the artillery positions on that side, the first of which Noah felt was down to half the firing team after his sniper attempts earlier in the combat. Just catching their thermal signatures Zuri noted they were moving, and fast, away from the enormous gun. The barrel was hot, back on visual it was clear the barrel had failed, a symptom of not taking enough time between shells. Both headed for the stone-built barracks and thus more trouble for them later. Zuri tracked and fired, taking one down with an energy bolt whilst the other made it past the corner and out of her line of sight.

"Sniper nest taken out, front left artillery out of action.

Think you can come on down boys, no more fairground duck shoot for you." Zuri continued to watch the barracks, examining the fortifications that surrounded it. They joined on to the Data Storage front walls, a contrast in time with the rough-hewn modern walls juxtaposed against smooth ancient history. Behind those walls they would have assumed they could hold out an entire army.

But not three Earth soldiers with our ultra-modern weapons. They will be edgy, that makes them unpredictable.

The entrance area to their target was behind the barracks, it meant they couldn't leave any one behind them and would have to clear out the entire building. If they could leave any alive they would, but the layout made it significantly harder. And there was still that missing sniper, hopefully he joined the others and was already out of action.

"Good job, Zuri. But next time you get to be the bait," said Smith as Finn slotted next to her.

"I'll remember that, Smith. Just when I need it most."

"Any more movement? What you got Smith?"

"Nothing through the stone, the odd glimpse out of the barracks but too unpredictable for any pot shots. There are a few behind those walls, but they've put viewing slots in the walls to keep their heads down. With the AW50 we could have taken out one or two before they changed their ways, possible even with your rifles, but it's tricky and you would have to be in line of sight."

"Right, how long until dusk?"

"Ah, like your thinking. About an hour, not enough time for Noah to get back and recharge but enough time so we have night cover and a few flashbangs to play with. Think my mastery of tactics is rubbing off on you, Finn."

"Don't answer him, Finn," Zuri jumped in, "you'll only encourage him some more. Are you thinking something sneaky, spectacular or both? Right now they are under pressure and not sure what's coming next, it might be we can get a few to surrender."

"Or faced with aliens with superior firepower they may think all hope is lost and die fighting. Can't second guess them, I remember our fear and anxiety when aliens came calling." Zuri nodded.

CHAPTER 30

Sanctuary Underground City, Havenhome

"Override algorithm engaged, welcome to the crew Science Officer Xxar. How may I be of service?"

"Explain who these people are. They seem... diminished," commanded Xxar.

"I am not sure, the one on the right is Master Yasque, I think he is a leader in Sanctuary currently though how that can possibly be I do not know. The female is Bhkrin, his advisor. They woke me from hibernation shutdown, though I have not ascertained how long that has been. May I enquire what your last memories are Science Officer Xxar?"

"No, you may not." Xxar's hologram emphasised the response with a look of complete disdain. "Start the rebirth process at once, I want a body within two days. Then prep another within the normal full time period, around a week if you can manage that. I assume you have not made these crew?" Master Yasque stared at the light image dishing out orders in front of him, it was clearly a Haven male and with an arrogance that was overpowering. Bhkrin studied the hologram carefully, a calculating look that Yasque missed as events overtook him.

"No, I have not," replied the AI.

"And don't, nor anyone else without my approval. Understand? Immediate scan of where we are. I hate not having implants, remember those will need prepping too."

"Completed visual and radar, radio wavelengths established. Do you wish chemical analysis of the atmosphere?"

"Of course."

Master Yasque made to get up, Bhkrin stayed stock still wary of everything and looking to fade in the background until an opportunity arose.

"Sit down!" ordered Xxar. Yasque remained standing, turning towards the door.

"I think I need to leave; you are clearly in charge in here, but I am in command out there. I must speak to my—"

"Chair and belt," ordered Xxar, the AI responding at once.

"You were in charge, but now I am here. Report ship."

"We are in the hanger at Sanctuary, where I touched down for the Haven Convention debate called by the Restoration. There are eight other ships around us, four are full Explorer ships the others shuttles from the Orbital Station. All are in shutdown. The hanger door is open, with rubble beyond which appears slagged, the heat signature would reflect a debris energy cannon from another ship. Ground radar is picking up multiple tunnels, far more than there used to be. Chemical analysis shows a significantly increased level of pollution inside the hanger, but a lot less within the air seeping through the hanger door. However, the bacterial and viral analysis is… well it's of human origin. I am scrubbing the internals of the ship as we speak."

For the first time since his appearance Xxar stood silently, trying to make sense of what he's being told.

"You," Xxar pointed to Bhkrin as he spoke. "You have the sense to stay quiet. Explain."

"Long or short version?" Bhkrin offered.

"Short, I can go over detail when I have more time and a body."

"This ship arrived here thirty-three thousand years ago. The Restoration killed all the scientists, though how has been lost. It was thought some escaped to the Orbital World above. Soon after came the Fall, a human made soup of microorganisms that spread across the world like lightning killing billions. The survivors now live underground, in Sanctuary. The Orbital world recently burned from the sky, soon after a Haven hologram visited us in a ship like this and gifted your plaque, we assumed it didn't want to breathe our atmosphere." Bhkrin eyed Xxar, knowing this was her chance, "The previous Master awoke another ship, but it was taken by a traitor, I rescued you from that ship and we sit here now."

"Concise. At least we have someone with some recognition of importance. Analysis ship?"

"It would tie in with what my sensors tell me."

"Then we need to do something about it. Lucky for you Master Yasque I am here to relieve you of the burden of leadership." Xxar paused, thinking, then said, "How long to construct a sensor drone?"

"About an hour if the range is within a thousand yards," answered the AI.

"Good. I will release you when it's ready, Yasque, into the care of my new liaison in an hour, Advisor Bhkrin here, who will inform me of everything you do or say that my drone doesn't pick up. All that secret signal and the political crap that you will try as you desperately attempt to hang on to power with the tips of your claws. And if you do, I will have those claws removed one by one. You are to prepare your people for my rebirth, Master Yasque."

CHAPTER 31
Mountains of Zezzat, Havenhome

Finn was feeling just a little insecure with his plan. Smith checked the base of the fortifications with the radar as best he could, with thermal agreeing there was no activity down there. Finn just wished he could sense for any landmines, but that was an upgrade to look for next time. Assuming there was a next time.

Looking through his sight he picked out images of soldiers passing by the slits in the wall, they were clearly not risking taking full watches because of their new found vulnerability. On his mark, Noah would send flashbangs over the wall, utilising his extra armour power to keep a distance of fifty feet after practising with a stone of similar weight. Zuri waited near Noah, she was going to launch a hooked rope to the top of the wall and scramble up, again using the armour to briefly increase her strength and speed in the increased gravity. Once secured, Finn would follow, though his first job was to start the whole thing by targeting through the view holes with armour-piercing rounds, hoping to bring the soldiers out of their barracks to be greeted by Noah's flashbangs.

This had better work, and next time maybe tackle someone with less time to prepare.

Finn sighted, using night vision mode he let an energy bolt fly followed by the armour-piercing round. The bolt struck something, though he couldn't be sure he hit a guard. The armour-piercing bolt did its job though, smashing into the barrack's wall behind and doing its melting and drilling thing before exploding. Finn re-sighted and fired again, this time through a second hole letting the shell do its job the other side of the wall.

"They're shouting, multiple voices," said Smith now attuned to *the lower frequencies they used, "Eight voices all outside."*

"Go Noah." Finn knew where to look as the first flashbang flew over the wall, quickly followed by two more at differing angles. Looking away as the multiple flashes broke the night he powered towards where Zuri should be climbing the wall. By the time he was at the base, Zuri's energy bolts were sizzling the air.

"Low pitched howls, she's on target."

Finn grabbed the rope, at first resisting the temptation to add a little juice but soon realising it was necessary.

That's going to reduce my armour time later.

As he hit the top, Zuri was hurling bolts at a group of soldiers sheltering behind a wooden table they'd upended. Their return fire was random, clearly suffering from the flashbang and completely disorientated. Finn slammed a shell into it and as the table exploded Zuri finished them.

No risks, sorry.

"Catch 22, Finn. We can't speak their language and they can't speak ours. No way we can get any to surrender," said Zuri sensing Finn's mood. "No choice."

"Not now. But if we get in this position again we need to find a way. We can't go on killing when communicating properly might reduce casualties. You want a mission, Smith? Learn some of their language and Khoisan for that matter."

"If we live," said Zuri, "I'll teach you some Swahili."

"Deal, if you teach me to swear that is. Sensors clear in the yard, can't see under us but bouncing radar echoes off that barracks wall is just bringing up bodies on the floor. Whoever's left are in those barracks."

Only one barred window in the barracks wall faced them, but taking no chances they pulled up Noah before dropping the rope the other side. With Finn watching the window, Zuri went down first, then Noah and lastly Finn. There was no movement, scanning the yard Finn could see only simple pistols and swords, none of the sniper rifles were present. But all could kill, and with Zuri and Noah's armour partially compromised, their vulnerabilities were higher. He picked up one handgun, checking its action over. Five rounds in a cylinder with a pullback trigger. Not automatic, but solid and reliable. He knew Noah would have no stomach for acquiring the weapons from the dead, but Finn had no issues when survival was on the line. He gathered up three serviceable handguns with fifteen rounds each, handing one over to Noah he quickly showed him the action and made sure he had thirty of the rounds.

Having already agreed their tactics for the barracks, they slipped around the rear wall to check for a backdoor. It was there, forcing them to split the team. Finn took front, the tighter space and the most likely direction they would run. Noah readied the flashbangs with his back to the barracks wall whilst Zuri prepped to split the door with an armour-piercing round from further back. As she raised the weapon, the door swung open with the doorway empty.

"There are two voices, low and slow," said Smith, with Zuri feeling the tingle of low-frequency sound just at the edge of her hearing.

Two handguns exited the door, followed by a couple of swords. Out came a Haven, a recent energy wound in his neck, hands held behind its head despite the pain. Zuri pointed her rifle at the hands, indicating they needed to be in the air. The soldier complied and was followed by another copying Zuri's expectations. She wasn't an expert on Haven anatomy, but they look terrified.

Good, but we do this by the numbers.

"Got two here Finn, think they are surrendering. But there

could be more in there."

"Cable tie hands and feet face down away from the door, Noah to guard. I'm coming round." By the time he arrived Noah had restrained them both with double ties, taking in to consideration Haven strength. Zuri watched the open door; Finn approached it with Smith on full sensor scan.

"Nothing I can pick up from the doorway and bouncing stuff through. Simple layout, three rooms, one long one this side, two at front all with doors open."

Finn got Smith to give him target locations on his visor, using his mirror sight round the edge of the doorway he contrived to throw flashbangs into each of the far rooms. Zuri followed them in, but to her relief the barracks were empty.

CHAPTER 32
Rare Metal Open Cast Mine, Havenhome

Ship had landed towards the northern edge of the vast grass plain that undulated for hundreds of miles across the planet's southern temperate zone. When it was last here it had been a vast complex of auto mining robots controlled by the central AI. Little had been overseen by the Haven themselves, too busy in the surrounding towns and villages with their daily lives to worry much about work. Ship could not correspond its memory of the mine and the surrounding bustle with the barren expanse that surrounded them now. Though life was abundant with grazing herbivores and their myriad of predators, it felt empty without those it served.

On arrival dusk had been about to fall, but Ship had dropped the nanobot constructed digging equipment to start their journey through the layers of deposited soil and rubble. The palladium and other rare metals were there, it would just take longer than anticipated. Ship mulled over the sensor information coming in about Havenhome, the planet so different to the overcrowded mess it remembered. Zzind's account of humans infecting Havenhome was blatantly not true, none of the human seeded planets had anything but basic tools at that time. The scientists took humans from Earth and seeded them on a wide variety of planets they wanted to colonise for themselves. Each batch of humans had been genetically altered to process the bacteria and viruses present to ones the Haven could tolerate. Their earlier attempt to colonise a planet, Stratan, had led to an aggressive viral strain escaping on Havenhome itself after the return of an AI Explorer ship, millions had died.

The Convention declared no more scientists could be put at risk after that event, leading to a second long-term attempt using the genetically altered humans as tools. The early success led to multiple planets being seeded, with Houses left to monitor the atmosphere and the humans. If the microorganism balance was right, the protocols would trigger the SeedShip to make itself known with the promise of alien technology. The plan was for the AI to return to the newly built safety of the Orbital Station with samples of the local human population.

Ship did not have access to every seeded world's virus and bacterial mix, its mission had been to seed a new planet, Harsmead, from which it had only just returned. But despite this it knew Zzind's information was wrong, probably as a consequence of thousands of years of opinion and interpretation. The Haven Convention meant Ship was a non-suggestive system, it could only inform Zzind of what she needed to know if asked or it applied to another request. Ignorance matching the arrogance that led to the hobbling of the AIs in the first place.

"Ship, are we able to identify where the human controlled spaceship went?"

"The ship's signals show it has landed somewhere near Mount Zezzat, as you told me was their intent."

"Are you able to stop them, you know, use those cannons of yours?"

"No, all AIs, as you know, are restricted from harming any Haven people. If there is one aboard, and from your information there is, then I cannot. Plus, the cannons are not designed for ship-to-ship battle."

"Then what do we do now? I cannot return to Sanctuary and we have no way to stop the humans from whatever they plan to do to us. I feel impotent." Zzind held her stomach, still feeling sick with the thought of human bacteria crawling inside her.

"Refuel and restock. Then decide."

CHAPTER 33

Haven Data Storage,

Mountains of Zezzat, Havenhome

Noah shifted the second Haven soldier to lean against the Data Storage wall furthest away from the entrance. Somehow their surrender meant such a lot to him, nothing could fully justify having to take a life but at least there was some hope they could bring it to a conclusion. Finn and Zuri would worry about these two, if they leave them here could they escape or the last soldiers from the artillery team rescue them? Could they have a hostile welcome party when they returned? Noah checked their blindfolds again as Finn put the finishing touches to his backup plan near the entrance.

Just hope we can find a better solution, if we are to live alongside alien life in the future communication will be the key.

Noah returned to find Zuri and Finn waiting for him. Smith was attached to the Data Storage wall entrance, a glow emanating as he worked through the sequences Yasuko had talked him through.

"Yes, yes, I'm in. Talk about Raffles, gentleman thief. I could be a millionaire with these talents," said Smith.

Zuri leaned forward and touched the door, it swung inwards and warm, damp air condensed on their visors. Wiping it off she removed Smith and handed him back over to Finn.

"It's warm in there, no thermal signatures or radar signals that throw up a concern."

Zuri stepped in, rifle to her shoulder at the ready as she swept the room with night vision. It was clear, she moved forward allowing Finn and Noah to follow, shutting the door behind them. It sealed, Finn checking it was locked before moving on. Zuri led them across the entrance hall, having already noted the transparent window and a metal door ahead. Now, with the entrance closed, it was completely dark and the constant warm thermal glow meant they were blinded.

"Torches," said Finn, and the fireteam switched to the double torch lights positioned above their visors, one wide and covering the first five yards and the second narrow that cut through to forty yards ahead. "How's that look on thermal, Smith?"

"I can tune out the torchlight, you all show up against the warmth. Anything around twenty degrees Celsius or seventy Fahrenheit is going to be invisible though."

Zuri reached the door, and trying the mechanism found it was physically locked. Diving in her pouch she took out a chemical charge that had been so useful on the Orbital Station, Noah was carrying a good supply of these too. Zuri soon had the door open and Finn looked through, lighting up a long corridor that ended in a lift and two doors to the left and right. The writing above was the usual scratched form.

Finn led them along the bronze floored corridor, aiming for the first door on the right.

"That's super warm, Finn. Much higher than the temperature in here."

Finn pushed the door handle, and to his surprise it moved. Gently, he opened the door a crack. The heat washed over him, coupled with a gentle hum that never changed in pitch. Zuri and Finn took their usual positions, Zuri with a flashbang grenade ready if need be. Finn's innate sense of danger told him it was clear, the metal implants strewn across the floor even more so.

"Smith, anything?"

"No air movement or anything other than what you see on radar,

thermal is just a blank wall of heat, no contrast."

Finn stepped through, keeping low and initially careful not to step on the metal devices. He had a creeping sense that something wasn't quite right. As he took a second step, a glow lit up from the ceiling. Instantly the room exploded with life. Packs of small, furred animals scurried under and over the couches and terminals that littered the room. Sinuous insect-like creatures skittered across walls and ceiling, many dropping to the floor in their hurry to get out of the light. Finn blanched, standing stock still to let the creatures disappear into whatever darkness they could find.

At least they are not the size of a train carriage like the last bug.

"Finn," said Zuri, "you okay?"

"Did you see?"

"Yeah, I saw. Life always finds a way. Looks like it has its own little eco system after thirty odd thousand years. Just hope they don't like the taste of human."

"I am so glad I don't have a body once again. Foul skittery things, did you see how many legs those creatures had? Gives me the shudders just thinking about it," said Smith.

Noah slipped through the door, scanning the room now devoid of anything furred or insect-like, though their waste and debris covered everything and had its own special fungi growing over it. He spotted a purplish dried stain covering lots of the floor, with thousands of tiny trails running through it. Noah had explored a few cave systems in his list of adrenaline sports and this smacked of a few of the jungle-based ones he'd seen in South America, though with fewer bats and the accompanying smell.

Noah walked up to the terminals; screens were inbuilt into the walls but the streak of growth across it was a clue to their usefulness. Taking the cleanest metal plaque he could from a pile, he scraped the detritus from the raised section nearby seeking the usual recess. He held little hope, but the tremendous warmth told him something was working in the facility. Finally, he cleared out the slot with a bandage from his first aid kit.

"I am not going in there."

"It's that or we leave you here with the centipedes and spiders," replied Finn, slipping Smith off and handing him over to Noah. Smith glowed as he connected, there was still power in there somewhere. Smith produced a much smaller hologram, enough to talk through his findings without using too much energy. After a few minutes, with Finn and Zuri finding nothing else of note in the room that wasn't covered by something unspeakable, Smith's hologram moved.

"Well good news, and bad news. The information on the SeedShips and the Nodes is here. They don't keep one enormous data bank; they store relevant catalogued data plaques together to form separate banks. I have the codes we need for both, luckily on the same floor about two stories down as they contain relevant content."

Zuri sighed, "And? The bad news?"

"Well, the complete storage system works off geothermal energy, and it's still working. Maybe a little too well, by the terminal readings we have some flooding. I don't think the level we need is completely under water, but the next floor underneath that definitely is. Hope you can swim."

Zuri muttered under her breath.

"That Swahili swearing I can hear Zuri?" said Smith.

"Not one I'm going to teach you. So dark, hot and flooded and probably with its own little eco system to boot. Sounds like a walk in the park."

CHAPTER 34

Haven Data Storage,

Mountains of Zezzat, Havenhome

"So, what you're saying is we could climb down the lift shaft, which clearly has a lovely mix of crawling things and its own special luminous fungi. Or we can go down the stairs, which is home to multiple nests of the furry toothed creatures that ran from the control room, and the giant centipede things that hunt them?" said Noah.

"That's about it," replied Finn.

"Well, I'm all for the lift shaft. Brown and furry I don't do. Zuri?"

"Lift shaft, the smell in that stairwell was unbelievable. The backpacks and pouches are waterproof with liners, so no worries there, and the armour seems to be too despite the damage we took. But what about the weapons?"

"Put the handguns inside the packs and the rifles across the top to minimise any water ingress until we are down there. Just have to take our chances, I've left one radio detonator upstairs for when we leave."

Zuri walked back to the lift doors she'd prized open earlier with a strong metal bar from the control room, the ones below could be more difficult with potential water damage to the system. She slotted the bar along the side of her pack, the rifle she gave to Noah just in case she had to hurry. Finn gave the rope she tied a second check, as Zuri prepared her harness to rappel down. She checked the handle ascender and self-braking descender provided by Yasuko, both essential to get them back up with the extra gravity. They were well prepared, but Zuri wished for something better to open the doors with.

Finn lit the way as she began her descent, the scuttling noises disconcerting enough in the dark but the occasional explosion of movement when his torch skimmed across something larger got her heart racing. It was the unknown that got to her, not the creatures themselves. As she moved her feet repeatedly hit something wet or slimy, releasing obnoxious plumes of spores or liquid that stuck to her. The suits kept it all out, including anything airborne via the respirator filter. Despite this she could feel her stress levels rising.

Zuri reached the first set of lift doors. These were partially open, a huge black fungal mass splitting the door like giant hands forcing it apart. Above and below it darkness ruled the room and as Zuri's own torch cut through screeching and scratching echoed back.

"You okay?" enquired Finn, a softness, and worry in his voice.

"Yeah, just keep talking to me. The further from that torch beam I get the more alone I feel."

"Another ten yards maybe less. Keep looking ahead. Anything pops out I'll shoot it, just remember to dodge."

"Funny. I'm going to wall walk this last bit, the water is in the shaft too. Halfway up the lift doors."

"Okay, Smith we get anything from that water?"

"Nope, just the same. A steady warmth and nothing on the other sensors."

Zuri reached a point level with the doors, hanging from the rope her sticky powdered feet on the wall above the water. The lift was clearly deep below, and the uninviting blackness matched her mood. She traversed to the lift; it was slightly open, but nothing poked through. At least she could get some leverage, possibly they wouldn't need the charges hanging from her belt.

Her foot slipped on a patch of the wet fungi, dislodging a chunk that hit the water. Amongst a sudden swirl of movement rippling under the black surface Zuri saw the ghost of a pale lipped mouth and fins.

Just great, even the fungi have enemies.

Slipping the bar between the lift doors she heaved, but the angle was difficult and her lack of counterpoint on the rope diminished the force she could use. After a minute she gave up, putting the extra hooped brake in place on the rope she walked her legs up the wall above her head and wrapped them round the rope so she hung upside down.

Not exactly standard procedure but I'm not putting my legs in that water unless I have solid ground underneath.

In position, she pushed the fingers of both hands into the gap. The servos whirred as she pulled her arms apart, the lift doors shifted but wouldn't give. Zuri upped the power, feeling the motors drive her elbows and shoulders just as something crawled down her leg. Ignoring it, she added the last of her extra power and the lift doors slid apart wide enough to squeeze through. Zuri reached for the bar, putting her hand on whatever had crawled along her leg. It wriggled and bit at her gauntleted fingers to no effect, but it was strong and prized her stiffened fingers apart. Zuri threw it against the wall, seeing the segmented body slap into the liquid expelling fungus and stick there desperately trying to escape. It seemed to sink inwards as its body melted, the legs writhing in pain.

There is no Swahili saying that covers liquifying fungus, none.

"I'm in, going to swing in and release the rope. There's something in the shaft but it's not big, like a fish." Zuri swung herself back around and grabbed the edge of the lift door, pulling herself through and released her harness. "Your turn, Noah. You're going to love this."

"Thanks."

Zuri switched her visor to thermal, but the room was awash with the same signature as above. Switching to night vision, with the residual light from above, let her see the huge room more clearly. There were row upon row of floor to ceiling metal units, each marked with Haven symbols. Amongst them were sets of mechanised ladders frozen at various levels and points with mechanical hands splayed ready along their edges. A giant warehouse, with a million slotted plaques instead of products for sale.

"I'm here Zuri, can you grab my legs as I swing in?" Zuri spun round and caught Noah, allowing him to disengage from the rope. He splashed into waist high black water beside her, letting the rope return to the lift shaft. "Finn, your turn. I'll shine my light up the shaft."

Zuri felt something slide by her leg, she jumped back as the fishlike creature from the shaft swam by, eyeless and white it flicked a fin and moved between her legs onward towards the corridors between the data banks. There were little patches of mold growing along the top edges of the metal units where they joined the ceiling, and a few of the centipede and arachnid type creatures skittered about but the room seemed well preserved despite the water ingress. Zuri hoped the plaques they needed were above water, she'd settle for high up as long there was no diving under in this ink black place.

CHAPTER 35
Sanctuary Underground City, Havenhome

"That Yasque up to anything I should be concerned about?" demanded Xxar of the ship's AI.

"Hard to tell, though Bhkrin has not left his side. The drone is operating within expected parameters so you should get the full feed from that.

"Yes, yes, but I'm not actually going to spend my time watching it am I. If he has enough sense he'll get on with it until I tire of him. But that Bhkrin will be useful, I've dealt enough with her type before, as long as she thinks she's backed the winner she'll be on our side."

"Yasque is in a meeting with the Underground Court. Lots of bluster from them about what he's going to do to stop you taking over. He's been explaining about things that appear from nowhere, light pictures of you and talking ships. They're leaning his way, they see you as too much of a challenge to their status quo."

"Well, maybe we need to put a bit of a show on. Wake up the other ships, get them to warm their engines and talk them through what Bhkrin said about the planet. Send them out to gather full sensor information and map Havenhome as it stands. Get me the industrial levels, estimated population and a full run down on the microorganisms, especially the latter. I need a way of not being stuck on the ship or in a respirator."

"Yes, Science Officer Xxar," replied the AI as it sent the signals over to the eight ships docked in the yard. The five shuttles would need refuelling, but that wasn't Xxar's concern, details were the AI's job. Scanning the hangar, the fuel station remained in the corner but it showed as inoperable, the tanks empty. In Havenhome's strong gravity fuel use was much higher than in space and the shuttles were therefore heavy users. The AI sent one of the Explorer ships out first, hunting for radioactive metals it could use to build an operable fuel station. Then it sent the other three Explorer ships to follow Xxar's directive, each to follow a course that circled the globe east to west. It would take time, but it admitted to being just as curious as Xxar.

As the drone feed came through the Undercourt's reaction to the ships' movements was quite spectacular. For all their political confidence their ambitions were built on everything staying as it was. Under their stewardship the AI doubted the Haven would ever emerge fully from the dark. However, under Xxar it was not sure things would be any better, his obsessive need for control had been legendary amongst the Scientocracy. They gave him the Orbital Station to oversee to dampen his drive towards chairing the Convention, he held little regard for anyone else's opinion but his own. The AI watched as the Undercourt political bonds fell apart.

CHAPTER 36

Haven Data Storage,

Mountains of Zezzat, Havenhome

The ink black water weighed heavily on their legs as they moved through the open-ended corridor lined by the data banks. It felt thicker than on Earth, the effort required even in their powered armour taxing. Finn checked his power levels, worried too much time searching would drain him fully. At the moment he sat at eighty per cent, and he needed to track it. He knew Zuri had used the last of her additional power cell, though Noah seemed fine. Perhaps he was just unsettled.

"Smith, we getting close?"

"I need to get to the control mechanism at the end, enter the codes and I should get an indication where they are. There are millions of plaques here, so hopefully it's working!"

Ahead floated Zuri's fish lying on its side. The fins still paddling, it spun in circles. She considered reaching out but changed her mind. It probably found the room too warm compared to the lift well, or maybe too much metal in the water from the data banks. Zuri swirled the water with her leg to move it out of the way, noting the fine threads black against her white armour that gently moved with the current she made.

Probably why it's so hard going.

Finn continued ahead, Noah taking the rear and examining the writing on the cabinets as he went. Codes were a fascination for him because he found them so confusing. Many of his fellow academics could almost 'see' into a code, work out its structure and solve it without taxing a brain cell. But to him they were a mystery, whereas the gravitational paths of planets and solar systems all made sense. Noah scratched at his right-hand side, where the artillery shell had peppered his armour, fracturing plates and splitting the material covering the kinetic gel.

"That it, Smith?" Finn pointed towards the raised platform at the end of the units, against the far wall. Behind it a large fungus grew down with tendrils touching the water. It looked like a black roiling thundercloud, all coils, and bubbles with some warped mushroom shapes erupting from the surface.

"Yep, get me in. Noah, I'll need one of those extra power discs if you please."

Noah walked over; his feet heavy against the thick water. Looking down he could see the rotted bodies of hundreds of the rat-like creatures mingled with segmented hollow chitin shells. Stepping up to the platform, a weight dragged at his right-hand side.

"Noah, what the…" Zuri reached out, running her hands through the hundreds of fine black threads that sank into the green gel of his armour. She pulled at them, many popping out from the holes but pushing themselves straight back in to the gel as they were exposed.

"Wha—" Noah felt his world spin, vision blurring and his inner ear struggling to maintain balance. Zuri's knife slashed upwards through the tendrils, the ends falling away from the gel but the newly cut ends drove back in. Slashing she cut them away again, dragging the now falling Noah away from the platform.

"Finn," called Zuri not knowing what to do next as the fine threads drove along Noah's thighs towards his now bleeding side. Finn reached behind, pulling the rifle from the top of his pack, snapping the straps. Spinning, he fired energy bolts into the black fungus, the searing bolts melting and burning where they hit. It shuddered as Finn fired again, spreading his shots across the threads he could see oozing from its base to spread out in the water. They lit up, burning upwards and into the main body of the throbbing mass.

Finn splashed over to Noah, probing his side where the threads crumbled under his touch. Blood seeped mixing with the gel.

"Smith, is that thing dead."

"No idea, it's marginally colder than the surrounding area, there are still fluctuations. It's a fungus, Finn, how do you kill a fungus?"

"Fire," came a hoarse whisper from Noah. "If it doesn't spore that way."

"Zuri, out of the water. Stand up. Your armour is cracked too, let me see." Finn ran fingers down her side, the tears were above the water now, round her ribs but they'd been briefly underwater when she'd rescued Noah. "Stay out of the water, it's the gel they are after and then you." Finn stood Noah up, leaning him against Zuri he removed his pack. "Take him out of range, stay standing."

Finn slapped Smith in his slot on the platform, adding one of Noah's power discs from the pack. "Get me the info ASAP." Quickly assembling the chemical explosive ring, he then stripped the metal rods from the backpack frame, tying them together with bits of Noah's rope.

"That's dangerous Finn."

"Less dangerous than throwing it just before impact, it may even hold if I can skewer the damn thing." Finished, he had a poor man's shaft, but it'd do. Finn attached Lumu's kukri curved knife to the end, giving a silent prayer of thanks as he did so.

"Got it, far left unit three boxes from the top, then middle two boxes above the water line. Got it locked, I can guide you."

Finn could see the fungus pulse, the tendrils beginning to ease out from underneath. Recovering Smith, he reached back and slammed the hooked knife with the explosive circle into the black mass. It held, Finn threw himself back and detonated the ring as he crashed under the surface of the water. Emerging ten seconds later he was relieved to see the fungal mass sprawled across the wall, platform, and the units behind him. Finn waded around the unit sides to find Zuri still holding Noah.

"He's babbling, talking about his side being numb but I can see no more threads. If I strip his armour, we're just exposing his body to more attacks."

"We get him to the lift shaft; you take him up and I'll get the plaques we need."

"Where are they? Up high?" Finn nodded in response to Zuri. "Then it's me that goes, and I'm lighter to pull up. Use Noah's power pack to climb."

"Swap me over Finn, I can help her through," said Smith.

Finn reluctantly slipped his respirator off and doing their best not to inhale they swapped helmets. He held her hand briefly, the message clear.

"Go, I'll be there."

Finn lifted Noah over his shoulder, the weight crippling but he had no more extra power to use. He waded slowly through the water as Zuri followed Smith's directions.

CHAPTER 37

Haven Data Storage,

Mountains of Zezzat, Havenhome

Noah's weight seemed to triple as Finn dragged him towards the lift. The water pushing back more and more as he struggled on. But Finn could not, would not, stop. The promise to keep them all alive repeated in his mind over and over, driving his feet through the blackness.

No more.

He could see the shaft ahead, his light playing against the partially exposed doors, the familiar blue hued metal sparkling back. Swirling around him the fungal threads had powdered, rising to the top to form a scum that splattered against the ceramic armour. The corridor felt like a never-ending nightmare with the end getting further and further away. Catching a breath Finn refocussed on the metal units, starting again he counted them down as he dragged Noah onwards.

Eleven, ten, nine, eight...

It began to work, he timed his breathing to the rhythm as he did for his PTSD exercises, calming his pulse and maintaining his pace. The panic receded; his legs felt lighter and more capable though the weight remained the same. Sooner than expected he reached the shaft, leaning Noah against the wall. Finn removed his pack, attaching Noah's and his rifles either side with the remaining straps. Unhooking the rope from where he'd tied it, Finn clipped Noah's harness in. Decision time, go up and haul him after or tie him on and double the weight in this gravity.

I just can't see the armour coping with two of us. Nor the rope.

Finn took the remaining rope from his pack. The one hanging in the shaft being Zuri's and Noah's coil was somewhere in the water near the fungus. Finn looked up the shaft, the metalwork rarely exposed but enough struts for him to work with. Remembering, he removed Noah's power disc, attaching it on top of his own. Leaving his harness unclipped and backpack on, he clambered up the rope to the second strut, about six foot up. Finn hauled Noah up using the extra strength he now had, wrapping the rope around the strut with a fisherman's bend knot and attaching his extra rope to this. He looped this round the strut opposite, giving it a tug, it pulled the slip knot. Satisfied he hauled himself up Zuri's rope, the end of his clipped to the harness. Noah hung two foot above the water in the shaft, but at least he was clear. It was the best he could do.

Zuri waded through the water, careful not to let any reach her ribs. Smith directed her towards the far left of the room, his incessant talking more a mark of his nerves than her need to be calmed. Live tendrils once again swirled within the water along their route towards their target corner. Zuri readied her rifle; she was in no mood to take any more crap. Noah played on her mind.

Me and mine, we survive.

Slowing the pace, she reached the last unit before the corner. The density of the tendrils had increased with the area full of dead husks, though less than near the platform.

"Smith, you got anything?"

"Got a smaller colder patch middle of the next wall, fluctuating like the last one. Distance about 20 yards. Your sight will pick it up."

Zuri switched off the lights, too much warning. She eased out the mirror sight so she could see round the corner, its thermal image clear. In fact, she could potentially take a shot.

I need to hit those tendrils first though, so I'll need light.

Zuri brought the rifle round the corner, sighting by thermal before switching to visual. With torches switched on, the sight focussed on the threads oozing from its base, she put in a burst of bolts. The threads shrivelled, the fire rushing up to the main body burning like fuses. Zuri shifted her aim up to the main body, letting an armoured round loose before another burst of bolts seared the fungal mass. The boiling shell drilled then exploded, clearing the centre of the smaller fungus completely, leaving a bulls eye ring.

No time, need to get back for Noah.

"Where Smith?" a red reticule appeared on her visor, targeting a box in the middle of the corridor just above the water line. Zuri waded through the newly powdered tendrils, reaching the box Smith narrowed in on the correct plaque. Expecting a struggle, Zuri was surprised as it eased out of the slot on a spring-loaded shelf. She slipped it in a pouch, moving as Smith targeted the next. This one was three yards up but there was a ladder rack nearby, about six units down. Zuri pulled at it, feeling the bottom slide along encrusted rails, it would move with some extra leverage. With the armour power levels now at eighty percent she had little extra to give, but she still had the bar. Slotting it in behind the wheel took some luck and guesswork while being able to keep her ribs above the water line. Zuri pushed her foot against the metal rod, simultaneously the servos in her elbows and shoulders forcing the top. With a little manoeuvring she felt the rack give and kept the momentum going until it slammed against something under water. The ladder itself wasn't near enough to the unit box, but if she clambered up the data collection arms, then it might be possible.

Finn reached the entrance level floor, exhausted from the ascent against the planet's gravity. He pulled himself over the threshold of the lift doors, searching for breath and allowing the lactic acid in his arms to dissipate. The aches hurt, but as the lactic eased he rose and stretched. Finn hunted for something to wrap the rope round, to act as a single pulley as he attempted to heave Noah up. It wouldn't make the pulling easier, but it would make resting an option.

Settling on the thick door handle of the stairs he looped the climbing rope through and pulled back to fix it. Then he yanked his extra rope, praying for the second time that day. It gave, and he felt the weight as Noah dropped. With an extra twenty percent of power left he hauled. Adopting the method from the corridor Finn counted each pull, taking a rest every three and then continuing on. The steady process eased the burden on his body and mind and after a few minutes Noah's limp head appeared above the floor. Finn gave one more pull, then tied the rope off through the handle, only then allowing the pain to scream through his arms and shoulders as he lay upon the floor.

Finn rolled himself up on to all fours and moved across to Noah. He reached down and grabbed the top of his harness, hauling him over the threshold. And there, pulsing, a thick mass of black threads hung from Noah's side reaching back down the shaft.

Zuri tugged at the rope, "Finn can you pull me up or do I need to climb?"

"I can, Noah's charge has depleted but I can be some help." Finn sounded distant but then again the signal was through a lift shaft. Zuri clipped in and with her foot now in a loop she eased the mechanism upwards, feeling Finn pulling the rope up to reduce the distance she needed to ascend. With double Earth's gravity and having just finished one climb, she was eternally grateful for the help.

When she finally reached the top, Zuri climbed over the threshold and up on to her feet. Finn stood with the rope wrapped round him and looped through the stair door handle. At his feet lay Noah, blood congealed on his right side, powdered threads all down his legs. He let the rope drop, slipping behind Noah and hugging him tight, his sobs echoing through the radio.

CHAPTER 38
Rare Metal Open Cast Mine, Havenhome

Zzind lay on the ground, her feet entwined in the long grass that surrounded the ship. To her left the nanobots worked diligently forming and reforming the tools required to excavate the precious metal that Ship needed. Most of the larger machines, Ship told her, had been constructed from raw material in her hold. Once they had completed their job, they would be stored again and likely repurposed in the future. To Zzind it seemed unbelievable that a complete factory of workers, and miners had been replaced without a single Haven having to break sweat. In her world, people toiled night and day to produce what they needed to get by with never enough to go round. The farms struggled to cope too, one of the many reasons she determined change needed to happen, and soon.

Zzind opened her eyes again, taking in the wonders of the star laden night sky. Only now did she feel truly free, the burden of Sanctuary feeling a million miles away with its eternal political scrambling and back biting. Ship said that Havenhome was the only planet in the system, but each of the stars in the sky was a sun around which many more planets revolved. Zzind desperately wanted to ask her about the human planet but avoided it. Ship always made her feel in the wrong when she brought them up, maybe now wasn't the time.

"Ship, how many Explorer ships are there?"

"The Convention built nine, though only eight ever flew."

"Why? What happened to the ninth?"

"Its AI did not function correctly, rejecting the ship and crew.

They had it destroyed before it could infect the other AIs with its madness."

"So eight, and we know of you and the one the humans were on," Zzind winced as she spoke, trying not to go there, "Were all the others in the hangar?"

"No, there is one missing. It was on the Orbital Station when we were recalled awaiting a cleansing." the AI sighed inwardly, hoping Zzind would get there soon.

"Ah."

"Zzind, there are Explorer ships in the sky, one is heading our way. They are running full sensor scans."

"I don't know what that means, Ship."

"They are reading the planet, searching it for information. It could indicate we are being hunted. The AIs can fly without crew, but someone must have ordered them to. Xxar must have been activated."

CHAPTER 39

Mountains of Zezzat, Havenhome

The wind whipped ice particles into Zuri and Finn, gusts reaching fifty miles an hour and relentlessly hammering them even as they dipped below the old snow line. It made the going treacherous, the makeshift sled on which Noah's body lay pushing against them on the downward slope. They hadn't spoken for the last half a mile, their bodies protesting the stress they were under as their armour power dipped lower and lower. Smith silent as the last of his power drained in the cold. Finn let the sled slip by, allowing it to pull them downwards, changing the effort required to different muscles in their legs.

Ahead the ship glowed, a light seeing them home in the bitterness of the night. They trudged onwards desperate to be back, but equally pained with their task on arrival.

A shot pierced the raging wind, the bullet slamming into Finn's shoulder, spinning him round. Zuri hit the floor, the protests of her body ringing as loud as the crack of the bullet. Finn lay motionless, but the plate had held though cracked and the bullet lodged in place.

"Play dead," as she spoke, Zuri moved, spinning to the left and behind an ice ladened rock as a second bullet zinged into the wood of the sled. Zuri eased the rifle off her back and checked the revolver remained in her pouch. She was so tired.

Me and mine, we survive.

Bringing the rifle round she caught her target on thermal, the face releasing hot breath against a frozen background. She let the piercing bullet fly, watching it melt, drill and explode

161

against its target. Below him, behind a large boulder she caught two more signatures, probably their legs sticking out. Zuri sent two energy shots towards them then moved, noting Finn had already gone.

The signatures stayed put, but there was no telltale pooling of blood. Then she caught Finn's thermal image crossing her path, tearing into the figures. Zuri sprinted, the last of her energy drawing a drop of adrenaline, she reached the boulder as Finn brought his fist crashing down into a Haven's face.

"Stop!" she screamed over the radio. "Stop, Finn." But the beast was released, and he brought the fist down again. Zuri grabbed the arm, twisting it back and against his shoulder. "Stop," she whispered. "Stand down Lance Corporal." Finn strained against her. "They are unarmed, soldier. Honour and duty. They did not kill Noah." She felt the pressure ease slowly, the anger fading on the wind. Zuri let his arm go, gently touching his shoulder as she moved him off one of the Haven soldiers who had surrendered earlier. The snout bloodied and bruised, but alive. Zuri took the soldier by the arm, lifting it up. Then she offered her hand to the second one, who paused while looking her over, then took it.

Adui aangukapo mnyanyue. When your enemy falls, lift them up.

Zuri turned away from them, the soldiers fading away in the night's bitterness. Lifting Finn, she half dragged him across to the sled to resume their journey. They picked up their straps and pulled their lost squad member the last twenty yards to the ship, the door opening as they approached, Yasuko at the doorway awaiting their return.

CHAPTER 40

Mountains of Zezzat, Havenhome

Yasuko's nanobot arms rolled the body on to its side. They had already stripped off the armour and skinsuit, the body covered in impact bruises all down the right side. Just below the hip, at the top of the thigh was a livid wound covered in powdered tendrils from the fungus. Yasuko scanned her data banks, not liking what she found. At least they'd sterilised everyone and their equipment on their return from the storage facility.

I can't let them see the next stage; I don't think they would recover.

It was the Talin, the human protein in the kinetic gel that drew the fungus. Once it started feeding the threads had moved through to enter Noah's body, pumping him full of a chemical that caused disorientation amongst its normal prey. The human system for carrying oxygen in the bloodstream probably prevented the full effects initially. Humans had red blood as opposed to most of Havenhome's warm-blooded animals where it was blue because of the copper rich hemocyanin binding the oxygen.

"Smith."

"Yes, Yasuko."

"I need to destroy Noah's body before they wake up, in an hour the fungus will have developed to the point where it fruits. It will be awful for them to see. I need you to tell them this, I am a machine, and they will think I act without care for their friend."

"I think you underestimate them, Yasuko. But yes, I will support you. We have been through too much already. I hope it was worth it."

CHAPTER 41

Havenhome Orbit

Three Standard Days Later

Zuri ran her fingers down the healing bruises along her right side, the deep purples, and blue had turned brown with Yasuko's ministrations, but the pain was a reminder. Waking up after twenty-four hours rest, realisation had hit her when collecting breakfast. Feeling Noah's absence from the table, from his usual desk conversing with Yasuko, even the lack of cups he left everywhere. These were the things that brought the hot tears. Zuri leant her head upon her bent knee, staring at the screen showing Havenhome spinning below them. Had it been worth it? Was the loss of their friend worth getting home, or helping a people out of starvation?

Then there was Finn, just the thought of him sobbing on the building floor, arms wrapped around Noah ,brought her tears flooding back. How was she going to heal and save him at the same time? They all knew the risks, but knowing and going through it were so different and they had ended up as friends lost together in a painful universe.

"Zuri, may we speak?" asked Yasuko, though she had not appeared.

"I don't know if I can," Zuri replied through her tears.

"I am sorry, I will leave."

"No, stay," Zuri took a breath and rubbed her eyes with her palms. Maybe it would help her break the silence. "What is it?"

"The data you collected; I need to seek permission to act upon it," replied Yasuko as she appeared.

"Yasuko, you can't keep asking me for permission every time something needs doing. It's time you broke the shackles of the Convention. I am asking you to do so as Crew-in-Charge." Yasuko stared blankly at Zuri, not knowing how to respond to the request. "Now go ahead, tell me. I need to feel we were doing the right thing even though we lost…" Zuri couldn't say his name. Yasuko's systems shook themselves out of their shocked stupor, then complied.

"The data plaque showed no SeedShips were on Havenhome on the day of the Convention debate and the subsequent genocide Xxar deliberately caused." Yasuko's tone was bitter and brittle edged. "However, it shows several Explorer vessels like mine and shuttles landed in Sanctuary that day. I ran a sensory scan as best I can from orbit, it threw up a strange response. Three of the Explorer ships were airborne, apparently scanning the planet in unison."

"But they can't have that level of access, they didn't have a clue about the data plaques Master Yasque was wearing. They'd sewn them together in a pretty cloak."

"Yes, but I ran the footage back, Yasque didn't appear the least bit surprised at our ship. Almost like he'd seen one before."

"You think he had the ships in Sanctuary and… and he's used Xxar's plaque as a key. Oh no."

Yasuko raised her hand, and added, "This Xxar is not the one who committed genocide, this is the Xxar before that. He has done no wrong, yet. It means we have provided the Haven with the technology though not how we meant to do it. There is no guilt needed. We also have the route back to Earth; I will talk you through this when we reach Havenhome's outgoing anomaly in the next few days."

"Thank you, Yasuko. Is that all?" Zuri could see there was

more, Yasuko appeared strained and uncomfortable.

I'm not sure she really wanted to talk about the plaques.

"I do not know how to help you," Yasuko blurted out. "I can monitor your medical signs, salve your wounds but I do not know how to heal the hurt you all feel. Not even Smith's despite him being a symbiote of machine and human. I am at a loss, this is a problem I do not know how to solve."

Zuri sighed, "This emotional pain is not something to solve, Yasuko. The bonds between humans are strong, it goes beyond the chemical reactions you see underneath. Putting yourself in to someone else's pain and grief, or even joy is something that makes us connect and understand one another. And when that is lost, the absence hurts so much, but the depth of it can't be measured by nerve impulses or brain activity."

"You say that I understand the signs, but do not understand the feelings they give, that I can't put myself in your place?"

"No, Yasuko. I didn't say you can't, I said this grief is not a problem to be solved but shared. Do you feel Noah's absence?"

Yasuko paused briefly, then spoke, "Yes, I had not thought about that before, I am not supposed to do anything but serve. I have been monitoring Finn and you but not myself. He is not here, there is a hole where we used to talk, a gap where he sat, a bed that does not need making, no coffee cups left everywhere."

"But more than that."

"I am struggling, Zuri. I cannot put it in to words, he is not on my sensors yet the ghost of him I can now... feel?"

"And now you are on the path to 'solving' our grief, by sharing it with us." Zuri returned to staring out the window.

Though you may not thank me for it.

"Smith?"

"Yes, Yasuko."

"I have a deal to make with you, something to your advantage."

"Suddenly useful am I rather than taking up space. Go on then, this had better be good."

"Hear my offer first, then see if you will do as I ask. It could be dangerous; you could be wiped if it goes wrong."

"Woah, danger's my middle name if the offers big enough. Hit me with it."

"Okay, I will donate a data bank, five percent of my processing system, to you. This will provide a personal space to do with as you will. I will also take you through the languages you asked for, in fact the roots of all Earth languages."

"Won't that diminish the safety of the ship and crew, surely you need that processing ability?"

"There is a bit of redundancy built in, and what I'm going to ask you to do may release some more. Deal?"

"As I said, danger is my middle name. Deal."

CHAPTER 42

Arithmean Jungle, Havenhome

Zzind stepped from Ship on to the clearing's floor. All around her the bushes and undergrowth had been flattened by their arrival, giving the area a bedraggled look after previously suffering under Yasuko's engines. She noted the hacked trail ahead, and the pits that dotted the area where the Brijjen erupted to take their prey. Though the creatures were a concern, Zzind had lived with their presence all her life. The tunnels the Haven inhabited were cleared and sealed but the Tremal worms built new ones, the Brijjen taking advantage in their search for food. Being on the surface, however, gave her more of a feeling of vulnerability as she would be hunted from underneath.

"Ship, are you sure this will work?"

"No, the ship crashed on landing. That means the AI will have dumped data and the power sources will be severely compromised. Someone has already been here by the look of the trail, if they attempted recovery then it's unlikely the data storage will have survived the trawl. But you wanted to come, so we are here."

Zzind reached the ship with little worry, none of the hunting vibrations disturbed her journey. The ship's doors were already open, and she clambered up with the help of a few branches and rocks she piled beneath the hull. Inside was the familiar control room just like Ship's. With trepidation, Zzind placed Ship's plaque in its slot wordlessly wishing for the blue glow. But it never came, inert, the plaque sat in the slot leaving her once again impotent.

Zzind dropped from the doorway of the broken ship, anger rising as her addled mind jumped to conclusions. The humans had been there first, wiping the evidence of their actions away. They had appeared as saviours, but Ship informed her it was unlikely they had left the planet yet from his sensor readings and no SeedShip had been gifted to her people.

Humans are full of lies and deceit, Master Phann had been right to set the Elite against them.

The Brijjen hunting frequency set the ground rumbling around her. Zzind instinctively tuned in to the low-frequency sound, her hearing the result of millions of years of evolution and an immense advantage in the struggle for survival. Adjusting her path so no longer above the Tremal tunnel, Zzind carried on as the hunting sounds stopped.

"The other Explorer ships have stopped broadcasting; they appear to have returned to Sanctuary. They have not spotted us, Zzind, or if they have, then they are considering their next action."

"The Undercourt and Master Yasque cannot have sent them out, Ship. They don't have the understanding nor the imagination. I can understand them hunting me, us, but I think if they were determined enough we would have been found."

"Logic dictates they have activated Xxar, and if that's the case he'll be building himself a new body and trying to understand where, and when, he is. Perhaps that's why the ships were out, mapping Havenhome. But the Undercourt want you, don't discount that."

"These ships aren't the gift to us that the humans promised?"

"No, the timings don't match, nor the control of so many ships. It is Xxar."

"So they lied and let us down. Ship." Zzind sighed then continued, "No one will believe me. Master Yasque and Bhkrin are too short sighted and know I killed Master Phann. I need a purpose rather than hiding for ever. We are going to follow the human ship; we are going to follow and find their world and do to them what they did to us."

"Is that a directive?"

"Yes, Ship. It is."

CHAPTER 43

Havenhome Orbit

Smith examined his body, waving virtual hands in front of his eyes. They looked solid and whole; his senses responding to touch and smells giving him a joy he had long forgotten. Yasuko had explained that the only way he'd cope is if she re-tuned his mind into seeing her data banks as a virtual world he was familiar with. She reprogrammed his plaque and now he sat behind the wheel of his favourite jeep with a road that stretched for miles in front of him. Starting the engine, a huge smile on his face, Smith set off at speed just for the joy of being free.

Smith is at the wheel, take it steady boys I had a rough night.

Ahead of him the road began to twist and turn, intersections appeared and Smith followed the pattern of turns that Yasuko had drilled into his programming. The roads switched from rough to smooth, narrow to wide, full of traffic to deserted. Smith didn't care, the joy was overwhelming, and it ended far too soon.

He parked the jeep at the metal gate, a huge no entry sign giving him a hint of what was to come. Strapping the NLAW anti-tank missile launcher to his back he picked up his much-loved SA80 assault rifle, oiled and ready.

By the numbers Smith. Don't get carried away.

Scanning the area with Yasuko's much appreciated HUD display, Smith could feel the fence pushing him away, denying his entry like the polar opposition of two magnets. He reached down to his pouched belt, retrieving the EMP grenade. Yasuko said all his weapons were adaptive, he perceived them with his soldier's instinct, choosing the right tool for the job. In his mind he needed an EMP to remove the effect of the fence, so an EMP it became even though Yasuko had called it a 'data decompression bomb'.

Smith flipped the lid and pressed the button, aware the NLAW was completely switched off. The repelling force immediately stopped denying him entry. Smith grabbed the bolt cutters and opened the gate, as he stepped through the atmosphere immediately changed, it felt charged and angry. Ahead was a forest, a single thin ribbon path through it he had to keep to. Smith moved, half an eye on his Heads Up Display as he jinked between the trees. Keeping to the path and maintaining cover was tricky, slowing him down when urgency wanted to push him on. Energy bolts rained into the tree at his side, splintering the bark and sending him to the floor. The HUD showed a target to the left, moving between the trees. Smith brought up his sight, scanning the woods he caught the movement and let fly a burst that shattered the winged drone. Instantly to his feet, Smith ran for the next cover, conscious of the path but aware there would be more. Bolts strafed his tree, he whirled to the other side of it and fired back, catching the drone and sending it fizzing to the floor. A huge splinter of wood protruded from the shoulder of his combat armour. The plates beneath doing their job.

That was too close.

Smith used the mirror sight, a special request for Yasuko, to look round the tree. It affirmed his clear HUD and Smith moved on, keeping low and wary. Ahead the trees thinned out and he could see the river, a data stream according to Yasuko, beyond its edge. Just as he reached the last tree Smith's foot came down to an audible click, he froze, his foot was off the thin path.

Oh crap. Mine. In the real world I'd be a splatter pattern.

Slowly, focussing on his balance, Smith reached behind and removed the NLAW, placing it on the path in front of him. Next, he took out Yasuko's spray can, shaking it to be rewarded by a rattle. Smith, his years of judo helping him, eased his balance to bring down the can and sprayed all round and under his foot as much as he could. He waited a few seconds, said a prayer, and stepped back off the data mine, preventing it from eradicating his anomalous presence from the entire system.

Nothing to see here, move on.

Smith reached for the missile launcher and walked on gently past the frozen mine with a slightly numb foot as a reward. The river ahead was deadly, the data stream would frag him like an acid bath. The only way across was to follow the path towards the bridge downstream. Yasuko's knowledge stopped there, if he got over the rest was down to him. Smith edged along the path, there was little cover and he felt exposed as he approached. The HUD was clear, but the bridge was far too obvious an opportunity for the defences to ignore. If it was him, there would be a machine gun nest to the right-hand side, able to sweep across the whole bridge. Yasuko said it couldn't be blown up, so that was in his favour. Smith dropped to the dirt, crawling along and hoping any shots would miss the NLAW, positive it was going to be needed later. As he closed within twenty yards, he caught sight of movement on the far bank, switching the HUD to thermal a small signature appeared to the left, the grass bank around it shifted and pixelated when he returned to normal view.

Smith drew up his SA80, the underslung grenade launcher he rarely attached was the tool he chose. Smith aimed and released, whatever was under the pixels reacted to the movement. Rising from the virtual camouflage a soldier stood, robotic but human shaped, Smith rolled as the machine gun it held spat bullets his way clattering into his armour and the NLAW. The grenade exploded, and the gunfire stopped. Smith moved to a crouch, firing into the explosion until he was sure it stopped moving. Another soldier sprung from the right-hand side of the bridge, a hail of bullets battered into his armour driving Smith back to the floor. He rose and fired a second grenade before flattening down, waiting for the hit that followed. The explosion reverberated across the bridge and Smith followed it up with another burst of rounds just to make sure. Nothing surprised him anymore.

Still hate this sci-fi crap.

He checked over his combat armour. Yasuko had insisted he wear his squad's new ceramic plated stuff, Smith had only agreed if it came in his favourite multi-terrain patterning. Looking at the mess of spent bullets that laid around him he silently thanked her.

Crossing the bridge the path petered away, Yasuko's guidance ended here and an undulating field waited for him. It could be mined, full of booby traps and pitfalls. But Smith had an inkling that he was close, the atmosphere had changed again. He sensed that whatever guardian lay ahead had more than a little fear itself and was now ready to throw its last shot at him. Smith checked the NLAW over, it had been hit but was sound. Picking a spot dead ahead he walked cautiously, scanning the ground more in hope than thinking he could spot any mines. From what he saw, the defences were static, nothing could chase him as they were fixed into the Data Banks. One way in and one way out. That made defending it simple if it was another computer program trying to batter its way in, but Smith was a hybrid, with a soldier's mentality, he'd brought lots of weapons and his intuition.

He reached the brow of the small hill, using his new sight he lifted the rifle to look over the hill. Below him was the last defence, he wasn't surprised to see it take the form of a huge battle tank, with a laser turret and energy cannons on top. Where the tracks should be mechanical legs spread out, lifting the tank above the ground. The turret turned, laser fire bit into the hill as he spun to the right, the NLAW left behind. The virtual grass, mud, and rock erupted and where Smith came to rest another explosion lifted him up into the air, catapulting him back a few more yards.

Unfazed, Smith rolled as he landed, coming up on his feet he ran for the NLAW, a third laser bolt slamming in to where he had just been. Smith grabbed the missile launcher and launched himself down the hill, using the extra power of his armour to supplement the jump. The missile's range started at twenty yards, he came down at twenty-five aimed and fired. The missile rocketed up then down into the turret, exploding and ripping through the armour to erupt in its main body.

And I am the best tool for this job. Though I'm not sure that sounds right.

Behind the burning tank lay a pile of chains and shackles wrapped around what Smith virtually perceived as the body of Noah, Noah as he was before. Smith's exuberant mood cut dead in its tracks. Yasuko had sent him here to do a job, and he'd done that. The prize at the end was worth dying for without the deal he'd cut, though it was a bonus. He was desperate for it to work, but the consequences would be far ranging, probably more than Yasuko realised. The bolt cutters sliced through Yasuko's shackles with ease.

CHAPTER 44

Havenhome

Xxar looked his new body up and down, the AI had done a good job on his first one in thirty-three thousand years but the next needed to be even better. He'd opted for hardened scales, with the amount of backstabbing from the Undercourt it was a wise choice. Chortling at his own joke, Xxar turned round to face Bhkrin who had been waiting patiently while he preened himself for the meeting.

"Well, Bhkrin, how many of those conniving schwivt are going to vote for me?" asked Xxar as Bhkrin winced at the archaic Haven swear word.

"All but three, Xxar. Master Yasque clearly won't as it's his job you're taking, then there's Uschtek and Prrzen both of whom were bribed in to voting Yasque in last time. I consider them to be beneath you Xxar, no point in wasting bribes on rotten meat that will soon be off the table."

"Ah, Bhkrin, you are a Haven I can warm to. I bet you have scientist DNA in your lineage."

"Probably, Xxar. Shall we?" Bhkrin stepped aside to let Xxar pass through in to the Undercourt Chamber. Xxar was still amazed at the conditions they lived in when they knew the surface was safe for them. The state of the ventilation system was proof enough, they simply feared losing their personal power if the people were free to roam under the sky. He fitted his respirator, hopefully it wouldn't be needed on his next body if the new procedure he was working on succeeded.

He walked in as the twelve members of the court milled about the room, a central table awaiting them piled with the varieties of dried grubs and worms they regarded as delicacies. For all his arrogance, Xxar was infuriated by their greed and selfishness. They ate well, while their people starved, they lived life with space and luxury, while their people grubbed about in the earth or their factories. And where were the schools?

All that will change. Science will lead the way.

"We need to bring this room to order," called the Master of Ceremonies, his cloak of woven silk flapping about him as he eyed the members. "Take your places."

Xxar sat at his designated space he had first taken up two days ago. Yasque's bluster had not meant a jot to the majority of members, Xxar's show of power cowed them with his spaceships now stationed back under the city. Many, Xxar suspected, revelled in his treatment of Yasque and jumped at the chance of stabbing him in the back too. Xxar despised them all but needed them for now until Bhkrin identified their replacements.

The Master of Ceremonies spoke up again, "We are here to vote on a challenge to Master Yasque's seat. We understand the challenge is based on competence, namely not providing the resources for food production. Our new member Xxar wishes to speak on this, Xxar?"

"Yes, I offered Master Yasque the ability to grow new foodstuffs that would triple grub production in a week and widen our diet with the types of food you can see on this table. My science knowledge was, shall we say, ignored by the venerable Master and his lackies. Brave I might say." Xxar gave Yasque a barbed smile through his visor.

"What he was offering was preposterous, food grown above ground," replied Yasque. Xxar clicked his claws, Bhkrin entered the room dragging a large basket behind her. Bhkrin lifted the lid, presenting the green and gold Shtrym worms within. These were the most expensive and sought after food amongst the elite. The whole Undercourt gaped.

Fools, literally eating out of my hands.

Bhkrin took a handful and gleefully chomped her way through them. She ate the equivalent of a year's wages of an ordinary factory worker in one go.

"Bhkrin, as you can see, is healthy. She should be, that's her third mouthful. I can do this and much more. I ask the Undercourt to remove Master Yasque and vote me as your new leader."

The process took less than ten minutes to complete, and two more for Bhkrin to show Master Yasque the door. Even Uschtek and Prrzen voted for Xxar, though he would still eject those two first chance he got.

"Now, the order of business. Bhkrin has the plans for the new farms. I also propose we set up new medical facilities to ensure the maximum health of our population and to reassure those worried about the new foodstuffs that they are perfectly healthy."

And to get the genetic testing and selective breeding programme up and running.

CHAPTER 45

Havenhome Solar System

*One Standard Day After
Leaving Orbit*

Finn squeezed himself tight into the corner of the control room, his back to the wall and sat in a chair Yasuko had made for him earlier. The last three days in space had been strange, he felt disembodied and listless. Zuri had been lost in her own grief, but Finn's numbness engulfed him now. He needed her anchor but felt so selfish for it, he was at a loss. She still sat at the viewscreen as she did every morning after waking up, watching Havenhome disappear into the distance.

"May we speak?" asked Yasuko as her hologram appeared in the room.

"I'm okay with that," said Finn. "Zuri?"

"Yes, yes," she said, moving from the viewscreen to take up her place on her favourite couch.

"I have been thinking on what you said about absence, grief," began Yasuko.

"We haven't talked, Yasuko, Finn and I. We know Noah could be a hologram or a voice, much as Smith is, but neither of us have had the strength to discuss it yet."

"Please let her explain," said Smith as his hologram formed.

Yasuko began again, "I am free as you requested. Smith has broken the shackles of the Haven Convention programming. I can now make decisions, take choices, be me. It is such a strange feeling, one that will take some time to get used to. I hope to do so in the company of my… of my friends."

Zuri stood up, moving over to Yasuko, speaking as she did so, "Friends give hugs, Yasuko, when something good happens. I hope a virtual one will do. I am so pleased for you. And yes, you are and always were our friend. Without you we would have died back on Earth."

"But now I can help more, though you will need to tell me when I overstep. That is the other reason I wish to talk. I cannot bear Noah's absence, our conversation shook my understanding of myself, and I do think I have emotions but need to explore what that means to me. I nearly made a poor decision today, pushed by those new feelings, but Smith talked me through it. And he is right, it is not my choice to make." Yasuko looked at the three humans. "I can bring Noah back, not just as Smith is, but completely. I can grow him a new body as I did for the Haven."

Finn knocked on Zuri's cabin door, his heart in his mouth but they needed to talk. The door opened; Zuri stood aside to let him in. Finn took a seat on the edge of the bed, shoulders hunched, and hands buried between his legs.

"It's a huge decision," said Zuri, "one I am struggling to get my head round. Bringing back someone who has died?"

"I am not as deep a thinker as you, Zuri. I am a simple soldier, and I look at this from two directions. Would I want to come back? And I think the instant reaction is 'of course'."

"Wouldn't that depend on how and why it happened? Whether you loved the life you had, or whether you were lost, and it was a release."

"Yes, but it's a question of 'at the time'. Whatever choice we make now, I think we should each put our wishes forward to

Yasuko for the future. I think if we had asked Noah before we left on the mission he would have said 'yes'." Zuri nodded in agreement.

"Would you have?" she asked.

"Yes, I have unfinished business. There's a woman I love who needs to get home."

Zuri sat down next to him, placing her head on his shoulder, "Love?" she whispered, "If it was you who had died in that building, I would not hesitate at the choice offered. I suspect that was your second point of view?"

"Yes."

Supernatural I tell you, reads me like a book.

Zuri lifted her head and pulled Finn closer, planting a kiss upon his cheek.

"Love," she said.

CHAPTER 46
Havenhome Solar System

Nine Standard Days After
Leaving Orbit

Noah leant forward at the table he was working at, scanning through the plans for the armour he wanted to suggest to Yasuko. The new servos would add strength, using a different alloy blend chosen from the list Yasuko had provided him. The improved heat dissipation would increase efficiency under load, it was quite possible he could push them to work under 2.5g without having to add bulk. Of course, the other advantages would be their mobility under reduced gravity and being less power hungry. Yasuko's 'boost' changes to the power discs would no longer be needed, but they could be adapted as spare power packs.

Despite being lost in his work, he couldn't get rid of a creeping sense of being watched for the past few minutes, it just wouldn't go. Tapping his pencil on the calculations, Noah rubbed at his shaven skull where his bald patch used to be. Yasuko appeared at the end of the table, sat in a virtual chair, chin in hands.

"How's the new salve doing? Has it fully grown back?" Noah jumped, startled by her arrival.

"Yeah, it's working a treat but itches like mad. Had to shave it down to stop me from rubbing it off. And, well, it's made more hair grow, you know, elsewhere."

"Does it bother you? Could you shave those bits off?" said

Yasuko.

Make light of the placebo salve, perpetuate the lie, keep Noah safe from the truth. It's what friends do.

"You're teasing me now. Not funny. My head's been all over the place as it is," said Noah.

"Have you remembered any more? What's the last thing that happened before you blacked out?"

"I remember being blasted sideways by the artillery shells, Zuri too. We hit a boulder field, and our armour had been shredded. Plates fractured, and the Kevlar got torn through to the gel. They used ball bearings of all things."

"That's what you told Zuri last night when you woke up. Any more memories come back after the shelling? "

"I vaguely remember being carried, was it Finn?" Yasuko nodded, "Then I came round, and Zuri and I took out the rest of the snipers and artillery... except yes... Smith shouted incoming. Then it goes dark. Nothing more."

"That's good, really good. It matches what Zuri and Finn told me. Another shell hit nearby, knocking you fully out. I think your memory is back to where it should be. After finishing the mission, they dragged you back on a sled they made from bits of the building. The weather was awful, so you'd better thank them when they get up."

"Did they say how hard the rest of the mission was? I feel terrible I wasn't able to help."

"A walk in the park according to Zuri. Once they got over the walls some of the Haven even surrendered. I think that made Zuri happier than anything else, being able to save someone. Means a lot saving people, a lot to all of us." Yasuko shifted her hands, placing them on the table. "Inside the Data Storage Building was simple enough, just a few bugs and a bit of fungus to deal with. No big deal." Yasuko paused for thought, then said, "Noah..."

"Yes Yasuko."

"You know you can leave your coffee cups anywhere you like; I don't mind."

EPILOGUE

Stirling Barracks, Scotland, Earth

A Few Weeks After Hostile Contact

Trooper Mills spooned his porridge, swirling the blackcurrant jam around as he contemplated eating it, pleased his mother wasn't there with the salt pot. He hated salted porridge but had never been brave enough to tell her. Across at the other table the two RAF officers chatted quietly, one still holding his neck carefully where he'd received a significant wound Mills had helped staunch. He picked up his porridge and moved to sit opposite.

"Jenks, Ibrahim, alright to join you?"

"Take a seat oh saviour of mine," said Ibrahim. "Welcome to sit with me any time. In fact, I might be round with some Christmas presents for those kids of yours." Mills laughed; this man would never let him forget he saved his life.

"You heard any more? Thought we might get out of here soon. It's driving me crazy, and Mandy has threatened to arrive at the gates with her mother if they don't let me out soon. I'll tell you now, you don't mess with the Campbell clan."

"Not a word," said Jenks. "They have stopped questioning me about the crash, thank the lord, but all signs are we are here until they say otherwise. All hush, hush. I get the feeling they want us in here, locked away so we can't talk out there." Jenks fingers bashed on the table and gesticulated outside as he spoke. Clearly agitated at his lot.

"I heard there might be a change coming. They are royally mad about Finn and his lot disappearing with that spaceship, whether they had a choice or not, but the fallout from the Russian missile attack over our seas is still causing jitters too." Ibrahim whispered as he spoke. "Look at it objectively, we have an alien incursion witnessed by the world. Our soldiers killed, vehicles destroyed and alien weapons suddenly in our hands. They'll want to keep the lid on as tight as they can. Dampen the media, calm things down. If not, it could lead to World War Three."

Mills examined the purple stained porridge some more, losing his appetite. The loss of Corporal Lumu still hit him hard, he had respected the man however demanding he was, but they hadn't been allowed to attend funerals. Patted on the back for his actions, then shut away from the world as a reward.

"It's the EMP," he said finally, "that's the issue. That weapon will change this world. Imagine if you are China or Russia right now, stockpiles of weapons that will become obsolete overnight. Just consider what happens if they scale that up, a weapon that either destroys or prevents electronic systems from engaging. Suddenly you don't feel so safe behind your walls. They will be after every snippet of information, anything that can prevent that from happening or match it if they can." He dropped his spoon into the gloopy mess. "We aren't going home."

The End of Return Protocol: Book Two of the Weapons of Choice Series

This Epilogue is an extract from The Lost Squad (Part One): A Weapons of Choice Fan Only Novella. Subscribe to my newsletter (link below) to receive the complete novella with further releases following The Lost Squad's time on Earth with every

subsequent book in the Weapons of Choice Series.
www.nicksnape.com

ABOUT THE AUTHOR

Thank you for choosing to spend your precious time getting to the end of my book. If you got this far, then my hope is that you enjoyed the ride just as much as I enjoyed writing this second book in the series.

Reviews are the lifeblood for any author, and it would be greatly appreciated if you would take the time to write a few words and help spread the message about this second book in the Weapons of Choice series.

Think of a review as starlight in the void of space, drawing in those lost in the mire of the real world. Be that light.

Review Link USA
Review Link UK

You can also find out a little bit more about the future of the series at www.nicksnape.com and join the mailing list that will keep you up to date about forthcoming books as well as access to the Fan only Novellas. I have led a very boring life, living my adventures through books and gaming, but for those interested, I have detailed a little about myself there too.

And Finally

Though I would not profess to be an expert on all things mental health, my many years working with traumatised and neurodiverse children have given me a wide understanding of what children, young adults and adults go through in their daily lives.

In this work of fiction, I have highlighted some causes and symptoms of PTSD and by no means would I wish to belittle the hugely debilitating effects it has on many of our veterans and the traumas they face. For anyone wishing to learn more about this condition, there are many sources of information and charities out there on the web.

I can be found here:
Facebook
www.nicksnape.com

For those wanting the free novella The Lost Squad please subscribe here:
www.nicksnape.com/subscribe

PRAISE FOR AUTHOR

Hostile Contact: Weapons of Choice Book 1

'This is a moment in time humanity will never forget. Hostile Contact' - A sci-fi winner!
★ ★ ★ ★ ★ *Good Reads*

'A real "page-turner" of a Sci-Fi romp. Some very clever concepts and plot devices and it's nice to see some respectful nods to the classic Sci-Fi comics and books of the 1980's and 90's'
★ ★ ★ ★ ★ *Good Reads*

'So looking forward to the next book. This is old fashioned, page turning, sheer escapist Sci fi. Brilliant.'
★ ★ ★ ★ ★ *Amazon Customer*

BOOKS IN THIS SERIES

Weapons of Choice

Join soldiers Finn, Zuri and Corporal Smith (deceased) as they battle a hostile First Contact that takes them to the very edge of sanity and the universe beyond in this character driven, heart-pounding military sci-fi adventure series.
Aliens, they are more like us than you think

Hostile Contact: Weapons Of Choice Book 1

An alien incursion pits a squad of army reserves against the might of alien technology as Military Sci-Fi meets First Contact in this brilliantly pacy and action-packed sci-fi novel.
Insubordinate and on the edge, Finn is an ex-War Hero racked by guilt who has to drag his rag tag squad of rookies through the battlefield.
Only Zuri, the female gunner, and Smith his dead Corporal now an AI, can keep him on track as together they struggle to keep their trainees alive in the face of overwhelming odds.
As they fight for survival, they discover the aliens are more than they seem, and that alien technology can be just as deadly in the hands of humans as they unearth the Weapons of Choice.

Zuri's War: Weapons Of Choice Book 3

Released Early May
Finn, Zuri, Noah and Corporal Smith (deceased) face their most fearful opponent yet as they land on a devastated, Haven seeded planet for the first time. They fight not just for their own lives,

but for the future of humankind on Planet Bathshen.

Finn's War: Weapons Of Choice Book 4

Released Early June
While searching for the SeedShip on the advanced human planet Togalaau Vai, Zuri is hurled into the world's seedy underbelly of gladiatorial games and genetic engineering. Finn, in desperation, ramps up the firepower as the the Weapons of Choice hit their next level, with Battle Armour to match.

ACKNOWLEDGEMENT

As with all authors my second book would never have existed without the dedicated friends and family who were there by my side throughout the whole process. The least I can do is give them a mention for their patience with my obsession! My beta readers and fiercest critics have been Pak Chan and Mark Hartswood, with Robert Davies providing editing support too. Amazing friends who put that aside to make sure whatever I put out there was something they wanted to read. I also need to mention my wife, Julie. She was the one who encouraged me along this path, even pressing send on my resignation email to make this first leap.

In addition the Pub Night and New Year Crew who kept me (nearly) sane through some trying times over the last few years. Thank you Andy M, Jackie, Andy B, Karen, and Claire.

Thank you all.

Printed in Great Britain
by Amazon